Dear Reader,

Home, family, community and love. These are the values we cherish most in our lives—the ideals that ground us, comfort us, move us. They certainly provide the perfect inspiration around which to build a romance collection that will touch the heart.

And so we are thrilled to offer you the Harlequin Heartwarming series. Each of these special stories is a wholesome, heartfelt romance imbued with the traditional values so important to you. They are books you can share proudly with friends and family. And the authors featured in this collection are some of the most talented storytellers writing today, including favorites such as Roz Denny Fox, Amy Knupp and Mary Anne Wilson. We've selected these stories especially for you based on their overriding qualities of emotion and tenderness, and they center around your favorite themes—children, weddings, second chances, the reunion of families, the quest to find a true home and, of course, sweet romance.

So curl up in your favorite chair, relax and prepare for a heartwarming reading experience!

Sincerely,

The Editors

DAWN STEWARDSON

After spending most of her life in Toronto, Ontario, Dawn
has lived for the past ten years in Victoria, on Vancouver
Island, with her husband, John, and their two large dogs.
They all enjoy the mild climate, the ocean, hiking in the
mountains and the city's huge assortment of wonderful
restaurants. (The humans enjoy those in person, the dogs
via doggie bags.)

HARLEQUIN HEARTWARMING

Dawn Stewardson

The Shelter of His Arms

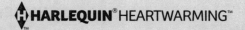

Recycling programs
for this product may
not exist in your area.

ISBN-13: 978-0-373-36615-6

THE SHELTER OF HIS ARMS

Copyright © 2013 by Dawn Stewardson

Originally published as THE MAN BEHIND THE BADGE
Copyright © 2000 by Dawn Stewardson

Printed in U.S.A.

The Shelter of His Arms

With special thanks to fellow authors
Linda Markowiak and Judith Arnold
for sharing their expertise.

To John, always

CHAPTER ONE

Sunday, October 3, 8:03 p.m.

THE UPPER EAST SIDE is arguably the best neighborhood in Manhattan and the old building was elegant—not the sort of place that would routinely have a crime-scene van and blue-and-whites sitting outside the entrance.

Travis parked behind one of the cruisers, then he and Hank climbed out into the gathering dusk and headed up the front steps.

"Homicide." He flashed his detective's shield at the officer guarding the door.

"Top floor," she told them. "Apartment 507."

As they passed the double row of entrance buzzers, he noted the gray residue of powder that said the buzzers had been dusted for prints.

Given the time elapsed, there wasn't much hope anything useful would come of it, but he was glad the crime-scene techs were being thorough.

On five, another uniform was posted outside 507. Yellow police tape secured the hallway in front of both it and the adjacent apartment.

"What's with the second apartment, Officer?" Travis asked, showing his badge again.

"It's actually one apartment with an adjoining office. The victim was a psychiatrist."

Travis nodded. "What else do we know?"

"Name was Steve Parker. Lived alone. Divorced, according to the next-door neighbor. And it looks like he was shot sometime yesterday."

"Nobody heard anything?" Hank asked.

"Well, our people are questioning the other occupants, but nobody called in a shooting. And in a building like this, if someone heard shots... I'd say the perp used a silencer."

"I'd say you're probably right," Travis agreed. "How about the doors? Any sign of forced entry?"

"Uh-uh."

"Who discovered the body?"

"The building manager. He had an appointment to see the vic about some repairs. And when Parker didn't answer his door..."

Travis nodded. "We'll want to talk to him, but we'll have a look inside first. The medical examiner arrived yet?"

"Uh-huh. Ten minutes ago."

When the officer turned to open the door, an all-too-familiar feeling of uneasiness crawled up Travis's spine. Even after four years in Homicide, walking in on a murder scene hadn't become routine to him. Each was different, and you never knew just how grisly any particular one would be.

This didn't seem too bad, he saw, relaxing a little as they stepped into the apartment. Nothing gruesome. Not at first glance, anyway.

A large, expensively furnished living room lay beyond the foyer—the body of a white, middle-aged man sprawled on the floor. Rob Gentry, an M.E. Travis and Hank had crossed paths with several times before, stood over it, making notes. A couple of the tech team members were methodically working away in the room. The others would be scattered throughout the rest of the apartment.

Hank closed the door; Gentry looked over and nodded a greeting.

Travis nodded back, breathing shallowly as he pulled on a pair of latex gloves. At his very first homicide, the coppery smell of drying blood had made him throw up. Since then, he'd been more careful.

"I hear he was a psychiatrist," he said to Gentry.

"Right. In private practice. His office area is through there," he added, gesturing in the direction of a hall that ran off the far corner of the living room.

"Forty-five years old, according to his driver's license." This time, Gentry gestured toward the coffee table. Its surface was clear except for a drugstore photo envelope sitting at one end and a wallet at the other.

"Wallet was in his bedroom," he said as Travis focused on it. "One of the techs brought it out."

The M.E. turned toward the body again and continued giving them details. "Killed last night between about nine and midnight. Four .38-caliber wounds to the chest from close range. Died almost instantly. Nothing indicates he was trying to defend himself."

"So he probably knew the killer. Had no concern about letting him in, then got taken by surprise."

"That's how I read it. Oh, and from the angle of the entry wounds I'd say the perp was quite a bit shorter than Parker. Probably not more than five-seven or -eight."

"Possibly female, then," Travis said to Hank. "That could explain why the vic was taken by surprise."

He nodded. "A .38's a lady's gun."

"By the way," Gentry said, "there's a contact-in-emergency card in his wallet."

Travis picked up the wallet, flipped through it and removed the card.

Originally, "Adele Langley" and "Mother" had been printed on the next-of-kin and relationship lines. That information had been scratched through and replaced with "Celeste Langley" and "Sister." The phone number had been changed, as well.

Absently, he wondered whether the mother had died or if Parker had just decided the sister would make a better contact.

"Langley, not Parker," Hank said, peering at the card. "Mother must have remarried before she had the daughter."

"Hey, you should be a detective," Travis told him.

He grinned. "Yeah, well, guess we'd better send a uniform to the sister's and let her know what's happened. Give me that number and I'll get an address to go with it."

As Hank took his cell phone from his pocket, Travis handed him the card. Then he walked over to one of the techs and asked if they'd come across an address book.

"Uh-huh. There's one in the end table."

"Good. If it hasn't already been checked for prints would you mind doing that right away? I'd like to take it with me. And there's got to be an appointment book in the office. Same thing with it. Oh, and if there's a Rolodex, it, too."

"Sure."

"Thanks."

He'd have to call Parker's Monday appointments and cancel them, then get one of the support staff to do the same for the rest of the week.

The apartment would remain a restricted crime scene until they were sure they had everything they needed. And he didn't want any patients showing up, expecting a session, and finding yellow tape and an officer outside the door.

After glancing around the room and seeing nothing else that grabbed his attention, he headed back across to the coffee table and picked up the photo envelope. The label on it was dated a year ago; the snapshots looked as if they were from a family gathering of some sort.

On the back of each picture, in the same neat printing as on the next-of-kin card, were the names of the people in the shot.

There were three of Parker with the same older woman. Printed on them was "Me and Mom."

After flipping past a few more pictures, Travis paused at one of "Mom" standing beside a much younger woman—an attractive blonde.

"Not bad," Hank commented, finishing his call and sticking the phone back in his pocket. "But her hair's too short."

Travis turned the photo over. It bore the words "Mom and Celeste."

"The sister," he said, just as the officer outside the door opened it and called, "Detectives?"

"Yeah?" Hank said.

"Got a minute?"

Through the doorway, Travis could see a second uniform in the hallway—clearly dying to tell them something.

"There's a guy who's been staying with a friend in 501," he began before they'd even stepped out of the apartment. "He came home around ten last night. And when he got off the elevator a woman was in the hall here, hurrying for the stairs. He'd never seen her before, but like I said, he's only a visitor."

Travis glanced toward the staircase at the end of the hallway. Few people on the fifth floor of a building would choose the stairs over an elevator. Not unless they were trying to avoid being seen.

"Did your guy have any idea which apartment she'd come from?" Hank was asking.

"No."

"Would you mind checking that out for us?" Travis said. "See if anyone on this floor had a female visitor last night. And if they did, get an ID and ask what time she left."

"Sure. But I already know nobody's home in a few of these apartments."

"Well, get answers where you can. And if nobody on five can tell you who she was, we'll want to ask *all* the occupants about her. How good a description do you have?"

"Not very. The guy only saw her from the back. But he figured she was in her twenties or thirties and..." The officer checked his notebook. "She looked 'stylish.' I don't know how he could tell that from the back, but it's what he said. She was average height, with short blond hair, and was wearing a gray trench coat. Had a big black purse slung over her shoulder. Or it might have been a briefcase with a strap. He wasn't sure."

Travis barely registered the last sentence. His mind had caught on the "short blond hair." He turned to Hank, reading his own thoughts in his partner's eyes.

There were probably half a million young women with short blond hair in New York City. Even so, instead of sending a uniform to notify the sister they'd go themselves.

CELESTE REREAD THE SENTENCE a third time. There was something decidedly awkward about it, but she couldn't quite figure out how to fix it. Finally, she gave up and set her pencil down on top of the manuscript.

She just hadn't been working up to speed lately—a serious problem when publishers always wanted a fast turnaround. However, past nine-thirty at night was definitely time to give up.

After switching off the desk lamp, she wandered from the spare bedroom she used as her office to the living room and stood staring down at the street, wondering how long it would be until she began to feel human once more.

Months yet, her friends had warned her. Probably a year before she was her old self again. She'd been close to her mother, so she couldn't expect to just bounce right back to normal.

Aunt Nancy had even suggested grief counseling, but that simply wasn't her. She'd always coped with her problems on her own.

Telling herself that things could only get better, she absently watched a black Mustang pull up in the No Standing zone outside her building's entrance.

The two men who climbed out were both tall, dark...and, yes, she'd give both of them handsome, too. They were somewhere in their thirties, and the driver put her in mind of Alec Baldwin.

That thought had barely formed before she recalled how annoyed her estranged husband used to get when she'd say that someone reminded her of a movie star. Bryce had always told her comparisons like that were stupid.

Of course, he'd thought a lot of things she did were stupid. Particularly toward the end.

As she looked down at the street again, to where the two men stood talking in front of the car, Snoops leaped onto the window seat and arched his back, demanding attention.

When she picked the cat up and cuddled him, he nuzzled his cold nose against her neck—his version of a kiss.

"Thanks, little guy," she murmured. "I needed that."

TRAVIS AND HANK had almost reached the stairs of the stately old brownstone when Travis decided the element of surprise would be a good idea. If they could simply knock on Celeste Langley's door, without giving her any advance warning…

"Let's wait outside a few minutes," he suggested. "See if we can get in without pressing her buzzer."

"Exactly what I was thinking," Hank said.

That was hardly a news flash. Hank was three years older than Travis and had been in Homicide longer. But they'd been partners for long enough that they generally thought alike—which was exactly what they'd been doing tonight.

During the drive over from Parker's apartment, they'd agreed there wasn't much chance his sister was their killer. Aside from anything else, they *never* caught the cases that were easily solved.

And even if Langley *had* been visiting her brother last night, it hardly proved she was a murderer. Parker could well have been alive when she left.

Still, you never knew what the element of surprise would produce.

"I'd say we just got lucky," Hank said as a teenager came along and started up the steps with keys in his hand.

"Excuse me?" Travis said. "NYPD detectives," he added, showing his badge when the kid turned toward them. "You mind letting us in?"

"I..." He glanced nervously at the gold shield, then shrugged. "Yeah, I guess."

They took the stairs and headed along the hall to 304, Travis not looking forward to what lay ahead. Informing the next of kin was never a fun job, so they took turns with the ones they did themselves. And this one belonged to him.

Hank knocked on the door, then held his badge up toward the peephole when they heard a faint noise from inside. "Police detectives, Ms. Langley."

"How did you get in?"

"Someone coming home."

"Do you have other identification?"

She was, Travis thought as Hank produced his photo ID, a typically suspicious New Yorker—which wasn't a bad thing to be.

A couple of locks clicked, then the door opened and Celeste Langley gazed warily out at them.

The snapshot hadn't done her justice. In living color, her eyes were the deep blue of sapphires. Her mouth was positively lush, and while in the picture she'd been wearing a tailored suit, tonight she had on a dark silk shirt and slacks that revealed slim curves.

Reminding himself why they were here, he said, "I'm Detective Ballantyne's partner, Ms. Langley. Detective Travis Quinn. May we come in? We need to talk to you."

For a moment he thought she was going to ask what this was about, then she simply stepped backward and ushered them inside.

Travis closed the door and followed her and Hank into the living room—wishing he were just about anywhere else. He knew she was assuming they'd come with bad news. People always did. But that didn't make delivering it any easier.

He glanced around as they sat down, doing

his standard quick assessment. The room, large enough to easily serve as a combined living and dining room, was tastefully decorated with quality furniture. The antique dining room suite was undoubtedly from the 1800s, or even earlier, and he'd guess that the artwork was worth a fair bit.

After taking a second to psyche himself up, he focused on Celeste Langley. "Steve Parker is your brother?"

"Yes…my half brother, actually." She paused for a beat, then said, "What's happened to him?"

"I'm afraid he was murdered last night. I'm sorry."

Her eyes filled with tears, and even though she managed to blink them back she suddenly seemed so fragile that Travis's heart went out to her.

That wasn't good, he told himself. He made a point of staying as detached as he could from cases. It went a long way toward helping him maintain his sanity. But, sometimes, keeping his emotions completely in check was tough.

"I'm sorry," he said again.

When Celeste nodded, he could tell she was trying hard not to let her tears escape.

After giving herself a few seconds, she focused on him again and said, "How did it happen?"

"He was shot. In his apartment. If it makes things easier, he died instantly."

"I...thank you for telling me that. And... who did it? Do you have any idea?"

"Not yet. We were hoping you'd be able to help us with that. Thought you might know if he had any enemies, or if there's been recent trouble in his life."

She slowly shook her head. "If Steve was having problems he didn't mention them to me. We didn't have the sort of relationship that...we weren't very close."

"He'd listed you as his next of kin," Hank Ballantyne said.

"Well, yes, I'm...I *was* the closest relative he had in the city. But..." Celeste paused. Even at the best of times, it was hard to explain that she barely knew her own brother.

"Steve's father was my mother's first husband," she continued. "After they'd divorced and she married my father, before I was even born, Steve went to live with his father. So he wasn't around much while I was growing up. And since he was fifteen years older than me..."

"I understand," Travis Quinn said, sounding so much as if he truly did that she tried to smile at him.

It didn't feel like much of a smile, but it was the best she could manage.

Then Hank Ballantyne was saying, "Ms. Langley, it's possible your brother had a female visitor shortly before he was killed. So just for the sake of elimination, I have to ask if you were in his apartment last night."

"No. I haven't been in his apartment since…not since our mother's birthday, back in March. And I wasn't anywhere last night. I mean, I was right here. Working."

"On a Saturday night?"

"Yes. I'm a freelance editor, and I have a deadline looming."

The detective nodded. "Okay, then getting back to your brother, when was the last time you saw him?"

"A few weeks ago. Our mother died in July, and after her service we decided we wanted to work on building more of a relationship. Neither of us had other siblings, so… Well, we had dinner together around the start of September and were going to make it a monthly date, but now…I…would you excuse me for a minute?"

She pushed herself up and headed to the bathroom, her tears making good their escape before she reached it.

Normally, she wasn't a crier. Her father had come from stiff-upper-lip English stock, and she'd learned early to conceal her emotions—especially from strangers. But first her mother's death, and now learning that Steve's life had been cut short, too...

They might not have been close, but that didn't mean she'd had no feelings for him. And the thought of someone murdering him had her completely torn up inside.

Leaning against the closed door, she stood with her eyes shut until she'd more or less regained her composure. Once she had, she splashed cold water on her face, wondering whether those detectives figured she was a basket case—then trying not to think she really might be.

Telling herself she was simply into emotional overload, she checked her image in the mirror and combed her fingers through her hair.

She looked as awful as she felt, as if she needed a month's sleep. But before she could try to get even one night's she was going to have to finish talking to those detectives.

Squaring her shoulders, she opened the bathroom door and walked back to the living room.

"I'm sorry," she said, pausing in the doorway. "My self-control is usually better."

"Don't worry about it," Travis Quinn said. "It's awful news to get hit with. And we won't bother you anymore while you're so upset. But if you'd just tell us one more thing?"

She nodded.

"With your mother and brother dying so close in time… Detective Ballantyne and I were wondering if there could be any connection between their deaths. So if you'd just explain how your mother died?"

That was hard to talk about, but she managed to say, "She was struck by a car. On Madison. The driver'd run a light and kept on going after he hit her. As far as I know, they haven't caught him."

Both detectives mumbled sympathetic responses, then rose.

"We'll want to talk to you again," Travis Quinn said. "Can we reach you here during the day?"

"Usually. Now and then, there's some reason for me to be at a publisher's. But I normally work here."

He nodded, then took a card from his pocket and handed it to her. "My cell phone's always on. If you think of anything that might help us with your brother's case, anything at all…"

"Yes," she whispered. "Of course."

"JUST WHAT WE FIGURED," Travis said after he and Hank had left Celeste Langley's apartment and were heading down the stairs. "There's not a chance in the world she'd ever murder anyone."

"Oh?" His partner shot him a questioning look. "You're sure about that?"

"You're not?"

"How tall would you say she is?"

"Five-five? Five-six?"

"Right. Average height. Wearing heels, she'd be maybe five-eight. And don't forget that Parker let his killer in. It was someone he trusted, someone he'd never have expected to shoot him."

"It wasn't her," Travis said firmly.

Hank shrugged. "I'd have liked a chance to check her closet for a gray trench coat. And a big black purse."

"A gray trench coat and a big black purse. Oh, yeah, I bet there aren't more than two or three women in the entire city who'd have both those items."

"Your sarcasm could use work," Hank told him. "Besides, our wit said it might have been a briefcase. And an editor would have a briefcase. Right?"

Travis ignored the question, but he was wishing he'd asked Celeste if anyone could corroborate her statement about being at home last night.

It hadn't been the time or place for that, though. The department didn't run sensitivity courses so their detectives would inform a woman that her brother had been murdered in one breath and make her feel like a suspect in the next.

Still, he'd sure like to know if she had anyone to back up her alibi.

He waited until they were getting into the car before he said, "You don't *really* think she could have done it."

Hank pulled his door shut, then looked across the front seat. "Well, she's blond, thirty years old, and I'd say the word *stylish* fits her. Then we've got the mother dying so recently—in an *accident.* If it turns out that Ms. Langley had anything to gain from those two deaths..."

"Hank, you're—"

"You know what else I think?"

"What?"

"That you liked her."

"I didn't *like* her!"

"No?" Hank did a poor job of concealing a grin. "Travis, how many people have we interviewed together?"

"I don't keep count."

"But it's got to be thousands, right?"

"Yeah, I guess. And your point is?"

"That I've never seen you react to any of them the way you reacted to her."

"What's that supposed to mean? *How* did I react?"

"As if you liked her," Hank said, no longer even trying to hide his grin.

"I felt sorry for her," Travis muttered, starting the engine. "That was all."

"Sure. If you say so."

Pulling away from the curb, he told himself to just let the subject drop.

Celeste Langley was an attractive woman, no doubt about it. But recognizing that was worlds away from being interested in her.

He wasn't in the market for a woman. And

even if he was, he'd *never* get involved with a suspect—whether she was an improbable one or not.

CHAPTER TWO

Monday, October 4, 8:36 a.m.

FOR THE TENTH TIME in the past half hour, Celeste picked up the card Travis Quinn had given her and checked the number of his cell phone.

Not that she needed to. By this point, she'd looked at it often enough that she had it memorized. Yet she wasn't sure she should call him this early. Or even at all.

Normally, she wasn't indecisive. But she'd had another sleepless night—lying awake unable to stop thinking about Steve and her mother. And it had left her so wrung out that she just couldn't stop vacillating.

Part of her brain was telling her not to impose on the man. Besides which, she hated the sense that there was no one she could turn to except a virtual stranger. On the other hand, none of her friends would have the answers to her questions.

Bryce would. Or if he didn't, he could get them.

She forced away those thoughts. Her estranged husband was the last person on earth she'd ask for help. Which really left only one option.

Telling herself she'd make the call brief, she reached for the cordless and pressed in Travis Quinn's number.

"Quinn," he answered on the second ring.

After taking a deep breath, she said, "Detective Quinn, it's Celeste Langley. I hope this isn't too early to bother you, but—"

"You're not bothering me and it isn't too early. What can I do for you?"

There was concern in his deep voice. It made her feel a little less anxious.

"Well, I didn't think of it while you were here last night, but…I should be doing something about Steve's death and I'm not sure what." Oh, man, she was sounding like an imbecile.

"There are the funeral arrangements to look after," she continued. "And I'll call the other relatives. But what about his friends?

"I met the ones who came to the service for our mother, and if I had his address book, I'm sure I'd recognize at least some of their names."

"You don't have to worry about contacting them. Detective Ballantyne and I will look after it. We have to talk to his friends, anyway—see what they know that might help. But can you recall even one of the names?"

"Yes. Gary Cooper. It stuck in my mind because of the movie star."

"Good. We'll start with him and he can tell us who else we should talk to. We'll inform your brother's regular patients, as well."

"And he was seeing a woman. You'll be sure to contact her?"

There was a momentary pause before Travis Quinn said, "What's her name?"

"Jill Flores. She was at my mother's service, too. I should have mentioned her last night when you said you thought Steve had had a female visitor. But my mind just wasn't working right."

"No, of course not. You were in shock."

"I...yes, I guess. But...even if you call the others, don't you think I should talk to Jill?"

"No, you shouldn't do anything. Really. Leave it all to us."

She heard the quiet sound of pages being turned, then Travis Quinn, said, "Yes, she's in his book. We'll get to her today. As for the funeral, you could make some tentative arrangements if you feel up to it. But until the autopsy's been done…"

The autopsy. Her stomach felt queasy. "When will that be?" she made herself ask.

"I'm afraid I don't know. Not for at least a few days, maybe even a week or so. Things are always backed up."

She closed her eyes, but that didn't stop her from imagining Steve's body lying inside a drawer in a cold, impersonal morgue.

"Ms. Langley?" Travis Quinn said when the silence lengthened. "Was there anything else you wanted to ask about?"

If there had been, the questions had entirely escaped from her head, so she said, "No, that was all."

"Well, as I mentioned last night, we'll be talking to you again. But if there's anything else in the meantime, don't hesitate."

"Thank you," she murmured. "Bye."

"Bye."

As she clicked off, Snoops turned from watching the sparrows outside and fixed her with a green-eyed stare.

"He seems very nice," she told him.

THE ICE MAN started the file printing, then let his thoughts drift back to last night's conversation.

"Hello. I got your number from Giovanni," the caller had said. "I was looking for…an exterminator. He told me you're one of the best."

"I'm *the* best." He smiled, liking that he'd had the chance to use that line again. It was a good one.

"Ah, I see," his caller had continued. "And he said you aren't *too* expensive."

"Depends on how tough the job is."

"It shouldn't be hard."

"Well, you tell me who and I'll check things out. Call me again. Let's say tomorrow night. If you like my price we'll get together."

"Good. But there's one other thing. You couldn't do it just any time at all. I'd have to let you know when."

"You talking *exactly* when?"

"No, there'd be a couple of days' time frame. I just don't know *which* days yet."

"Okay, not a problem."

"Fine. Then you want to check out a woman named Celeste Langley. She lives on West Seventy-fourth."

Celeste Langley. The Ice Man silently repeated the name he'd already grown familiar with, then glanced at the computer screen—thinking that modern technology was making his job easier all the time.

Used to be, he'd sometimes spend days just learning what he needed to know about a target. Now he could find out a lot of it on the internet.

Of course, that meant getting into the right databases. Ones with detailed information about people. And most of them were supposedly restricted. But if you knew what you were doing, privacy was a thing of the past.

He reached for the page his printer was spitting out and skimmed the facts again.

Celeste Langley. Thirty. Born and raised right here in Manhattan. Both parents dead. Separated from her husband. No car. Lived alone and worked out of her apartment.

That was going to bump his price up some.

A job was easier when the target had a regular pattern. Went out to work same time each morning and came home same time each night. Then you could just pick a place along the route.

Someone who worked at home, though… That might mean having to waste her in her apartment, and he didn't much like inside jobs.

Oh, he did them now and then, but more could go wrong. So maybe he should have a look at her place before he decided on his price.

He glanced at the address again. West Seventy-fourth.

It would be one of those old brownstones. Three stories. Not many apartments in the building. No doorman.

After thinking things over, he decided it shouldn't present much of a problem. So he wouldn't bother checking it out just yet. He didn't like to put too much work into something until he had the money in his pocket.

IT WAS A FEW MINUTES past four-thirty when Travis and Hank arrived at the NYPD crime labs for their meeting with Saban Mustac— head of the crime-scene team assigned to Dr. Steve Parker's place.

The techs had finished up early this morning, then he and Hank had done their own search through the apartment.

After that, they'd interviewed some of Parker's neighbors. They'd also seen Gary

Cooper and gotten a list of Parker's other friends.

Overall, they had a lot to go on now, which had Travis feeling far better about the case.

Most victims know their killers. That was rule number one in Homicide. And since Parker had let his murderer in, the rule undoubtedly applied. So after they finished with Saban, they'd get back to interviewing people. Starting with Jill Flores.

By this point, their team had established that none of the other residents in Parker's building had had a blond female visitor on Saturday evening. Which left little doubt that their mystery woman had been there to see him. And if Flores fit the description...

Travis glanced at Hank as they stepped onto an elevator, thinking back to Celeste Langley's call. When he'd told Hank about it, the first thing he'd asked was what Jill Flores looked like. And Travis had been really embarrassed at having to admit he didn't know.

He should never have forgotten to ask something so basic. And he found the reason he had very unsettling. Because the reason was Celeste Langley.

The instant he'd heard her voice his brain had gone fuzzy around the edges—something he couldn't recall ever happening with *any* other woman, let alone one on a suspect list.

The elevator reached six and stopped. As they started down the hall, he began wondering, yet again, whether Hank *seriously* figured Celeste could be their killer.

Tempted as he was to ask, he didn't. One round of Hank's "You like her" routine had been enough.

He hated it when his partner picked up on something faster than he did, which was exactly what had happened in this situation. He'd realized that even before Celeste had called.

After all, if he'd actually merely felt sorry for her last night, he'd hardly have woken up with her on his mind this morning.

When they reached Saban's cubbyhole of an office, the man was on the phone. He waved them in and cut his call short, then flipped open a folder, muttering, "Let's see, what have I got for you so far?"

Once he'd glanced at the notes, he focused on them.

"Okay, we lasered the vic for prints and fibers but came up empty. The door handles were nothing but smudges. There were a couple of prints other than Parker's in the kitchen, but I wouldn't get my hopes up. My read is that the shooter came in, did his thing and left. Didn't stay a second longer than he had to.

"We bagged a fair amount of trace evidence from the apartment—including a few hairs that obviously weren't the vic's. Plus, there's everything we vacuumed up. I've sent it all for analysis, so now it's a question of waiting to see what the lab boys make of it."

"What color are those hairs?" Hank asked.

"Blond."

"How long?"

Saban glanced at his notes again. "Four to five inches."

"Longer than your average male's," Hank said.

"Uh-huh. And the angles said the perp wasn't real tall. So maybe the he was a she. You've got a female suspect?"

"Two possibles."

Two. Then Hank *did* seriously think Celeste might have done it.

Travis checked his watch, telling himself that could well change when they talked to Jill Flores. Hey, maybe they'd *really* luck out. Maybe, when they told her why they'd come to see her, she'd admit she was their killer.

Of course, that was way too much to realistically hope for. But he and Hank were so overdue for a gimme of a case that you never knew.

CELESTE SPOONED OUT Snoops's dinner, then stood gazing into the open fridge, trying to decide what she'd make for herself.

She really had no appetite, but—

Her phone began to ring, delaying the need for a decision. When she picked up, Bryce's voice greeted her.

She swallowed hard. She had no appetite for talking to him, either.

"Celeste, Nancy called to tell me about Steve. And I just wanted you to know how sorry I am."

"Thanks," she murmured, guiltily thinking she should have called him herself. But when Aunt Nancy had offered to do it, she'd gratefully accepted.

She didn't like phoning Bryce at his office, because since they'd separated, his assistant always managed to make her feel as if she'd picked the worst possible moment.

And she liked calling him at home even less. The few times she'd had to—for one reason or another—his live-in girlfriend had answered.

"You've been having a bad time of it lately," he said.

"It hasn't been the greatest, but I'm coping."

"Good. You know...I hadn't talked to Steve since your mother's service. And, of course, we were never close. But...something really strange happened on Saturday evening."

When Bryce paused, she gave him the "Oh?" he was waiting for.

"Donna's in a play, so she was at the theater," he continued. "And I was home alone, catching up on some work. And...I got this feeling I just couldn't shake. One of those vague feelings that something's wrong, you know?"

"Uh-huh." Bryce was prone to vague feelings about all sorts of things.

"And something certainly *was* wrong."

She realized he expected a comment about his being psychic, but she simply wasn't in the mood to humor him any further.

"So," he continued when she said nothing, "you'll let me know when the service will be?"

"Bryce, you don't have to come."

"I feel I should. Unless it would upset you to see me."

"No, it wouldn't upset me, but—"

"Good. Then let me know. And if there's anything I can do in the meantime…"

"Thanks, but I don't think there will be. I made most of the arrangements today, so it's just a question of how soon the…"

"Autopsy?" he said.

"Yes," she murmured, certain she'd never hear that word again without thinking of Steve.

AS THEY NEARED Jill Flores's door, Travis suggested that Hank do the talking.

It was easier to concentrate on reactions and body language when you didn't have to think about the questions you were asking. And if Flores turned out to be blond, he didn't want to miss a thing.

Hank knocked. A few seconds later, a woman inside the apartment said, "Yes?"

"Ms. Flores? Police detectives." Hank held his ID up to the peephole.

The door opened—and Travis wondered if they would be lucky this time around.

She was closer to forty than thirty. But their witness had only seen the back of the woman in the hall. And Flores was "stylish," with short blond hair that was a shade or two darker than Celeste's.

"May we come in and talk to you?" Hank asked.

"What about?"

"It would be better if we came inside," he said.

The woman was clearly uneasy, but most people were when a couple of detectives appeared at the door. After another look at Hank's ID, she led them into the living room.

"We're here about Steve Parker," Hank began after they sat down. "I'm sorry to have to tell you this, but he was murdered on Saturday evening."

"Oh, no," she whispered.

Her eyes grew misty as Hank elaborated. When he was done, she murmured, "That's so awful. Sometimes I wonder why people live in this city."

After giving her a minute, he took his notebook from his pocket and said, "I'm afraid we have to ask you some questions."

"Yes. Of course."

"How long had you been seeing Dr. Parker?"

She hesitated briefly. "You aren't under the impression that I've seen him recently, are you?"

"We're only aware that you dated him."

"Yes, I did. But it was from early June until about a month ago. Then we decided things just weren't working out."

"I see. And have you had contact with him since?"

"No. We…well, we didn't see any sense in pretending we were going to remain friends when we wouldn't. So the end was the end."

Hank nodded. "What about enemies? Do you know if he had any?"

"If he did, he didn't tell me about them."

"And when the two of you called it quits? Did that have anything to do with another woman?"

"No, it was…basically, we'd just come to realize that we didn't have much in common."

"And what about another woman since? Were you aware that he was seeing anyone?"

Flores hesitated again before saying, "No. As I told you, there's been no contact. Not even a phone call."

"Well, the reason I asked is that we believe he had a female visitor on Saturday evening. Would you have any idea who it could have been? Did he have any women friends who might have just dropped by or—"

"You think a woman killed him?"

"We'd simply like to question his visitor. So, as I said, if you have any idea..."

"I don't. I'd like to help you, but I really don't."

Hank nodded. "I'm sorry I have to ask this, but just for the record, where were you on Saturday evening?"

"I was with a friend," she said slowly. "A female friend. She came over around seven, we had dinner here, then watched an old video. *The English Patient.* We're both Ralph Fiennes fans. And it's a long movie, so she didn't leave until after midnight. Do you want more details?"

"No, but I need your friend's name and number. Again, it's only for the record."

"Her name is Rhonda Stirling. And her number is 555-1623."

Hank jotted that down, then closed his notebook and thanked Flores for her time.

Travis added his own thanks, gave her his card and asked her to call if she thought of anything that might help them.

"Anything at all," he added before she closed the door.

"What do you think?" he said as he and Hank started down the hall.

"Same as you. Our wit put the blonde in

the hall around ten. M.E.'s estimated time of death is between nine and midnight. Flores was watching her video the entire time."

"You know that's not what I meant. Do you think she was lying?"

Hank shrugged. "Always a possibility."

"I've got a feeling that either she was or there's something she held back. And she knew Rhonda Stirling's number without looking it up. Which probably means they're pretty good friends."

"You're saying good enough that Rhonda might give her a phony alibi?"

"It wouldn't be a first."

"Yeah, well, we'll check it out. But at this point Flores is a whole lot lower on my list than Parker's sister."

Travis frowned. He and Hank rarely had different gut reactions to people, and he'd be a whole lot happier if they'd read Celeste Langley the same way. As in, innocent.

They reached the elevators and silently waited—until Hank caught his gaze and said, "I was right last night, wasn't I. Something about that woman got to you."

He shook his head. "I told you, I just felt sorry for her."

Hank eyed him, clearly not buying that. But

when he spoke again he simply said, "Good. 'Cuz I'd hate you to start feeling anything more, then discover she's our perp."

A LITTLE BEFORE TEN, Travis and Hank called it a night and started uptown, heading for Manhattan North Homicide so Hank could pick up his truck and get home to Jersey.

He had a house on a couple of acres, not far from Madison. It was a bit of a commute, but he'd bought there because his ex-wife had wanted to live in the "country." They weren't there long, though, before Jane left him. Like so many cops' wives, she just hadn't been able to take the night work and impossible hours.

They made marriage a risky proposition for a cop, and one Travis intended to continue avoiding—despite his mother's hints that thirty-three was more than old enough to be settling down.

Turning his thoughts back to their newest case, he began mentally reviewing the evening.

They'd made six stops after leaving Jill Flores and had caught five more people at home. Three of Parker's friends and two of his long-term patients.

All had professed shock at hearing he'd been murdered. Each had seemed sincerely upset. None had told them anything helpful.

Of course he'd given them all his card, so there was a chance that one of them would think of something useful and get back to him. Or maybe a detail neither he nor Hank had picked up on immediately would fall into place later.

That often happened. One person you questioned said something that eventually came together with what another one told you.

Adding up bits and pieces was how you usually solved homicide cases.

He turned onto East 119th, and as they neared the parking garage, he asked Hank, "What do you want to do in the morning?"

"Sleep in."

Travis grinned. "I can live with that. How about I see you here at ten?"

"I could probably manage nine-thirty. That would let us talk to a few more people on our Parker list, then spend the afternoon playing catch-up."

"Sounds like a plan."

Despite the pictures Hollywood painted, big-city homicide detectives didn't have the luxury of devoting all their time to a single case. He and Hank routinely had more of them on the go than they could reasonably juggle.

They reached the garage and his partner climbed out, then turned to give Travis a tired wave. As he disappeared into the garage, Travis started back downtown.

One of the good things about both living and working in Manhattan was you were never very far from where you were going. Which meant that in mere minutes, barring a traffic crunch, he'd be home.

Just as he was debating whether the first thing he'd have when he got there was a hot shower or a cold beer, his phone rang.

Hoping it wasn't someone calling about a fresh homicide, he dug the phone from his pocket and answered it.

"Detective Quinn, it's Celeste Langley again."

Instantly, he felt the edges of his brain growing fuzzy.

"I'm so sorry to phone this late, but—"

"Don't worry about it. I barely finished working," he said, thinking she sounded upset. "In fact, I'm still on my way home."

"That's a very long day."

"Yeah, it is."

"I...Detective, I just had a call from a man who told me he was one of Steve's patients."

Travis felt an icy numbness at the base of his spine, the sensation he always felt when he knew he was hearing something *not* good.

"He said that you and Detective Ballantyne had been to see him, and—"

"What was his name?"

"Evan Reese."

Definitely not good. Reese had been seeing Steve Parker five days a week for the past three years, but he was clearly a long way from being cured of whatever his problem was.

Not that Travis figured he was any expert in the field of psychiatry, but it didn't take Sigmund Freud to recognize a mentally unbalanced person. And his read on Reese was that the man might be dangerous.

"We talked to him a couple of hours ago," he said, keeping his voice calm. "Why did he phone you?"

"He said he wanted to offer his condolences. But...well, the thing is, the conversation got weird enough to make me nervous."

Weird. Crap. They were well beyond not good.

"Even so, I wouldn't be calling except that I

simply couldn't figure out why you'd tell him about me, let alone give him my number. So I decided that if I bothered you for just long enough to get an explanation, I'd sleep a lot better."

"Ms. Langley…did he *say* we gave him your number? Or are you only assuming—"

"No. He said you happened to mention Steve had a sister, and that when he told you he'd like to offer me his sympathies you gave him the number."

"Well, he lied."

"You mean about your giving him my number? Or do you mean you didn't even mention me?"

"Not a word."

"Oh," she murmured.

Her tone told him he'd just upped her anxiety level.

"Then how did he even know I existed?" she asked.

"Your brother must have talked about you."

"No, that can't be it."

"He wouldn't have had to say much."

"But he wouldn't have said *anything*. I wasn't an important part of Steve's life. I don't imagine he ever talked about me to anyone, and he'd definitely never have said a word about his personal life to his patients."

"You're sure?"

"Yes. It would have been inappropriate, and one thing I do know about Steve is that he was very professional."

Okay, if it wasn't Parker who'd told Reese...

Travis tried to think of another possibility but came up empty—probably because his mind was so closely focused on the fact that since Reese had Celeste Langley's number he likely had her address, as well.

That thought reminded him he'd forgotten to ask an obvious question, so he said, "Regardless of how Reese knew about you, is your number listed? Could he have gotten it from Information?"

"Uh-uh. It's unlisted."

"Then I think we'd better talk some more about this face-to-face. I'll be there in five minutes."

"No, wait. Coming here at this time of night would be crazy. I can—"

"Five minutes," he repeated. "Ten, max. And..." He hesitated.

What would happen if Reese showed up at her place?

He considered the question for a couple of

seconds, then decided that when she'd been so cautious about letting him and Hank in last night, she'd never open her door to a stranger. Especially not one like Reese.

And that meant there was no point in warning her not to. It would only make her more upset.

"And what?" she said.

"Nothing. Nothing that can't wait till I get there."

CHAPTER THREE

Monday, October 4, 10:23 p.m.

GAZING OUT INTO the night, stroking Snoops's soft gray fur while she watched for Travis Quinn, Celeste couldn't help feeling a little dumb for not even considering that Evan Reese might have been lying.

If that possibility had occurred to her, she'd never have bothered Quinn. But she had. And despite her guilt about that, she wasn't entirely unhappy that he was on his way over.

She was feeling a chilliness that had nothing to do with the room temperature. If Reese hadn't gotten her number from the detectives, then where?

And how had he even connected her to Steve when their last names were different? Obviously, he'd somehow learned Steve had a sister, but just how had he honed in on her?

While she anxiously watched the street, a car sped down it and pulled to an abrupt stop in front of her building. A black Mustang. The car Travis Quinn had been driving last night.

A sense of relief enveloped her as she watched him climb out. There was something about him that she found extremely reassuring. Something in addition to his being a cop.

In part, she knew, it was simply that he looked like a man accustomed to taking charge. He moved with a fluid confidence, and his features, regular as they were, were decidedly masculine.

But there was more to it than that. And although she hadn't managed to put her finger on exactly what it was, she'd caught herself wondering about it a dozen times during the day.

All she felt certain of was that it had to do with the way he'd watched her last night. She'd been aware of his eyes on her almost the entire time.

Strangely enough, it hadn't made her uncomfortable. In fact, it had made her feel as if he was on her side.

Oh, she realized that didn't make sense. He and his partner had simply come to tell her about Steve. There'd been no question of "sides." Yet, whether it made sense or not, that was how she'd felt.

She continued gazing down at him until he'd walked halfway up the front steps and disappeared from view. Then she hurried to the entrance hall.

"Hi," she said, pressing the intercom button after her buzzer sounded.

"It's me."

"I know. I was watching for you."

Once she'd released the downstairs lock, she opened her door so she could wait for him in the doorway. A minute later he strode out of the stairwell and started along the hall toward her.

He was taller than she'd remembered him. And even more attractive. His dark eyes were the color of rich chocolate, and the little laugh lines around them were appealing.

Appealing. Her choice of that particular word surprised her.

Since her marriage had fallen apart, she'd only been aware of good-looking men in the abstract. And thinking in terms of "appealing" was moving from the abstract to the concrete.

Be careful, she warned herself. The last

thing she needed was her thoughts wandering along those lines.

"I feel terrible about dragging you over here so late," she said, gesturing him inside.

"You didn't drag me—I insisted. And the time doesn't matter. There's nobody waiting at home for me, and if I cared about nine-to-five, I wouldn't be a cop."

"Well, even so... Can I at least get you something? Coffee? Or soda? I don't have any beer."

"Do I look like a beer kind of guy?"

"Aren't most men?"

He smiled. She smiled back, aware it was the first time she'd felt like smiling all day.

"A cold soda would be nice," he said.

He trailed along as she headed for the fridge. When she turned to set the cans on the counter he seemed to have completely filled her little galley kitchen with his presence. It made her far more aware of him than she felt comfortable with.

Telling herself a second time to be careful, she reached for the tab on the first can.

"Want me to do that?"

"Sure. I'll get the glasses."

By the time she had, he'd opened the sodas.

He poured them into the glasses, then followed her into the living room.

"So," he said as they sat down. "Tell me more about Reese's call."

She hesitated, suddenly afraid that once she had he'd think her phoning him had been downright silly.

"You said the conversation got weird," he prompted.

"Well...yes, it did, although it started out normally enough. I mean, I was surprised when he introduced himself as one of Steve's patients. But if he'd simply said he was sorry about what had happened, I probably wouldn't have given his calling a second thought."

"He said more, though."

"Yes. First, he got into how awful the timing was for me—with my mother having died so recently."

"How would he know about that?"

"I assume Steve told him. I know I said he'd never talk about his personal life with a patient, but he canceled some of his appointments after the accident. So, if he canceled one of Reese's I guess he explained why."

Travis Quinn nodded for her to continue.

"Initially, he just seemed concerned about me. But then he began getting personal."

"Saying…?"

"Well, for example, he asked if my father was alive. And when I said that he died a few years ago, Reese said he certainly hoped I had *somebody* to lean on.

"I suppose that sounds innocent enough when I repeat it, but when he said it…"

"How did you respond?"

"I told him I had some really supportive friends. Then I wondered if, instead of that, I should have said I was in a serious relationship."

"Are you?"

"No."

She waited a beat, half expecting him to tell her how *he* thought she should have handled it. When he didn't, she said, "At any rate, the next thing he asked was whether I lived alone, and that was when I *really* began getting nervous."

"And you said…?"

"That there was no need for him to worry about me. That my building's very secure and the neighbors all watch out for one another."

"Your building isn't bad. Is the part about the neighbors true?"

"Not exactly. The ones I've met seem nice

enough, but I barely know them. I haven't lived here long."

He didn't ask for more details. However, his expression said he'd like them, so she added, "I left my husband in January and took a sublet while I looked for something permanent. I've only been here since June."

"Ah." He slowly rubbed his jaw, which drew her attention to his four o'clock shadow and reminded her how long a day he'd had.

"Detective Quinn—"

"Travis," he said. "Why don't you call me Travis."

He hadn't even spoken all the words before he began wondering what he was doing. He was here because he was a cop, not to get friendly with the woman.

She looked a little surprised, but smiled and said, "Call me Celeste, then."

Nodding, he told himself he'd only suggested they drop the formality because it felt strange to be sitting here drinking soda with her and calling her Ms. Langley. It had been nothing more than that.

Sure, buddy. Let's be honest and admit you like her.

The imaginary voice sounded so much like Hank's it almost made him smile.

Of course, he didn't know her well enough to really *like* her yet. But he'd admit to finding her attractive. After all, he'd been admitting that—to himself, at least—since last night.

And the fact that he did was hardly surprising. Her smile was fantastic. And she had a beautiful mouth. Basically, she had a beautiful *everything*.

It made him curious about what sort of idiot her husband must be—to have given her reason to leave him. But that was *not* what he should be thinking about.

Scrambling to remember where they'd left off, he said, "So, getting back to Reese, you told him not to worry about you and then...?"

"He said he couldn't help it. Because... This was what *truly* scared me. He said the two of us are cosmically connected."

Travis felt that icy numbness at the base of his spine once more. "Cosmically connected. Did you ask exactly what he meant by that?"

"Uh-huh. And he said part of it was that I was an editor and he was a writer, so we were like two halves of a whole. But, far more significant, I was Steve's sister. And Steve had been a very important part of his life. Which meant we had to look out for each other. So he'd keep in touch."

Terrific. Just what she needed.

"Travis, he left me with such a creepy-crawly feeling I didn't know what to do."

"Well, you did the right thing by phoning me."

"Then you don't think I overreacted?"

"No. In fact, I'll pay him another visit to-morrow. Make it clear he's not to contact you again."

"Really?"

"Uh-huh. *Reduce fear* is one of the man-dates in the department's mission statement." Not that he was going to worry about reduc-ing Reese's fear. He'd threaten to hang the guy up by his ears if he ever called her again.

"I'll get back to you after I've talked to him," he added. "Let you know how it went."

"I'd appreciate that."

He pushed himself up, knowing he'd better get out of her apartment—pronto.

Until he and Hank were certain she hadn't killed her brother, she was a suspect—regard-less of whether he believed she could have done it or not. So he had to leave before he did something even more stupid than telling her to call him Travis.

CELESTE LOCKED HER DOOR, then resisted the temptation to head straight to the window so she could watch Travis as he left the building.

Instead, she sat down with her still half-full glass and asked herself what on earth was going on.

Her life had been heavy on emotional turmoil lately, and until she started feeling a lot closer to normal she'd be crazy to even contemplate getting involved with a man. Yet she couldn't deny the tug of interest she felt toward this particular one.

Likely, she decided, that was the "something" she'd been trying to put her finger on all day. Last night, she'd been so upset she hadn't consciously realized she found him attractive. But tonight had been a different story.

After he'd said there was nobody waiting at home for him, the statement had lingered in her mind. And she doubted he routinely asked people he was interviewing to call him Travis.

Snoops skulked into the room and leaped onto her lap, deciding it was safe to come out of hiding now that the company was gone. She began to stroke him, her thoughts turning back to Travis.

She felt immensely better than she had earlier, and that was entirely due to him. She'd told him what was bothering her and he'd come up with a solution. He'd talk to Evan Reese and set things straight.

It had been a while since she'd had someone offer to take care of a problem for her. And clichéd as it might be, she really did feel as if he'd lifted a weight from her shoulders.

Of course, as he'd said, it was part of his job. But even so, she had the distinct sense that he was going above and beyond for her.

I just hope you have somebody you can lean on.

Thinking of Reese's words again made her wonder if that could be what she was doing with Travis. Was she *leaning* on him? When he was a virtual stranger? Who'd only come into her life because he was investigating Steve's murder?

After considering the possibility, she decided she'd better give a lot of thought to exactly why she was attracted to him. Because not doing so could be very dangerous.

WHEN HIS PHONE rang at seven-thirty Tuesday morning, Travis groaned and pulled his pillow over his ears.

He hadn't gotten home from Celeste's until midnight. Then he'd tossed and turned, unable to sleep because visions of her kept wandering through his brain.

That had started him wondering whether someone could have hypnotized him without his knowing—and given him a post-hypnotic suggestion that was keeping her constantly on his mind.

Deciding whoever was calling wasn't going to give up, he grabbed the phone from the bedside table.

There was a moment's silence after he answered, then a woman said, "Detective Quinn, this is Jill Flores. You and your partner came to see me yesterday. About Steve Parker."

"Yes, of course." He sat up in bed, trying to force away his grogginess. "What can I do for you?"

"First, I should apologize for calling so early. But I wanted to do it before I left for work. I don't have much privacy on the job."

"That's okay."

She didn't continue immediately, so he said, "Did you remember something that might help us with the case?"

She cleared her throat. "It wasn't really

something I remembered. I just didn't mention it yesterday."

So his sense that she was holding out on them had been right.

"Then I started thinking I'd better tell you," she added.

"Good. You never know what will prove useful."

"Yes…well, your partner asked if Steve had been seeing anyone since we broke up. And I said I had no idea, but that wasn't exactly true.

"A couple of weeks ago, he asked one of my friends out. One he met through me. I only knew about it because she called to check that I wouldn't mind.

"At any rate, she's seen him a few times. I didn't say anything about her last night because she's the sort of person who'd get upset about being questioned by the police. So since I knew she couldn't possibly have been involved, I didn't see the sense in putting her through it.

"But after I'd had time to think, I realized Steve might have said something to her that would give you a lead."

"I'm glad you reconsidered," Travis said,

grabbing a pad and pencil from the bedside table. "And her name is…?"

"Ah…do you think you could avoid saying that *I* told you about her?"

"No problem."

"Thanks. Her name's Beth Winston. I'll give you both her office and home numbers."

He jotted them down, then said, "And she works…?"

"On Wall Street. For a law firm called Mitchell and Conlin. She has her own office, so if you wanted to talk to her there I think it would be all right."

"Great. And thanks a lot for calling. I really appreciate it. By the way, just out of curiosity, what color is her hair?"

"Oh…about the same shade as mine. Why?"

Another blonde.

Resisting the temptation to ask if Beth owned a gray trench coat and a big black purse, he said, "Oh, it really *was* just curiosity."

After saying goodbye, he put down the phone and glanced at the clock. If Beth Winston started work at nine, he had enough time to be there waiting when she arrived.

That would make him late meeting Hank,

but he wouldn't care. Especially not if this woman turned out to be their mystery blonde.

He phoned and left a message for Hank at the precinct, then got the coffee started and headed for the shower.

Barely half an hour later, he was climbing into the Mustang. Not many detectives drove their own cars on duty, but he'd had enough bad experiences with ones from the pool that he always did.

Despite the morning traffic, he arrived at the offices of Mitchell and Conlin before nine. Even so, Beth Winston had beaten him there.

"Is she expecting you?" the receptionist asked.

"No."

"And your name?"

"Travis Quinn," he told her, thinking he'd only say he was a police detective if he had to.

Since Beth Winston was the type of person who'd get upset at being questioned by the police, she'd probably get even more upset if her coworkers knew about it.

The receptionist didn't press him. She just buzzed Beth, then directed him to her office.

When he reached its open door, the woman

behind the desk said, "Travis Quinn? Should I know the name?"

"No."

He handed her his card, then appraised her as she eyed it.

Maybe thirty-five and definitely "stylish." She might well be their woman. And there was a gray trench coat hanging on the coat-rack in the corner. Seeing it started his hopes climbing.

When she looked at him again, he decided Jill Flores had been right. He hadn't asked a single question yet, and Beth Winston already seemed upset.

"Would you like me to close the door?" he said.

"Please."

Once he had, she gestured for him to sit down and said, "I assume this has to do with Steve Parker."

"You've heard, then."

"Yes. One of his friends called me last night."

"I understand you were seeing him."

"I'd been out with him three times. And I…" She paused and shook her head. "I could easily have been with him on Saturday. He asked me to a movie, but I already had plans.

"My sister moved away from New York last year, and she was coming home for a week. So I'd asked a few of her friends over."

"To your place, you mean."

"Yes. Just an after-dinner thing. Drinks and catching up. You know."

He nodded.

She had an alibi. He'd check it out, of course, but she was probably telling the truth.

"Except for that..." she said.

"You would have been with Steve Parker."

"Yes. I can't quite get over it." She nervously drummed the surface of her desk for a couple of seconds, then murmured, "What time was he killed?"

"Sometime between nine and midnight."

"Then if I'd been with him he'd still be alive. We'd have gone someplace after the show." She shook her head, looking close to tears.

"I liked him," she said at last. "It's very sad."

"Yes. It is. And I'm sorry I have to make you talk about it, but I need to ask a few more questions. Have you ever been in his apartment?"

"Only once. And just briefly. We stopped by because he had to get something."

But she *had* been in it. So those blond hairs the techs bagged might be hers rather than the killer's.

"Is there anything you can tell me that might help with the case?" he said. "Was Dr. Parker having problems with anyone? Did he ever say something was bothering him? Anything at all?"

Watching her slowly shake her head again, Travis wondered how many dead ends he'd hit since he'd earned his shield. But there was no value in dwelling on that.

TRAVIS TURNED into the Manhattan North Precinct's parking garage and began watching for a space. After he found one, he headed inside.

Hank looked up from his desk as he approached and said, "What's been happening?"

"Jill Flores called me first thing—to tell me she actually *did* know who Parker'd been seeing lately. So I paid the woman a visit."

"And?"

"She turned out to be a blonde with a gray trench coat. But she has a solid alibi for the time of the murder. I got the names of the people she claimed she was with and called a few of them on my way here."

"And aside from that? She have any ideas for us?"

"Nada."

Hank's shrug said *You can't win 'em all.* "So, what do you want to do now?" he asked.

Show time. Travis didn't want to tell his partner about going to Celeste's place, but he had to. "We've got to talk to Evan Reese again," he began.

"Oh?"

"Yeah. I had a call from Celeste Langley last night. Just after you headed home."

Once he'd elaborated, Hank said, "You figure that was a smart move? Going to see her without me?"

"What should I have done? Called and told you to turn around and meet me there?"

"No," Hank said slowly. "But you could have just gotten the details over the phone."

"We know Reese is a nut bar. And he scared the devil out of her."

Hank shrugged again.

"So I stopped by. Her apartment was practically on my way home, anyhow. You've got a problem with that?" he added when Hank said nothing.

"How long did we work yesterday? Twelve hours? Thirteen?"

"More or less."

"Well, if anyone else had called at that point, I doubt you'd have headed right on over just because she was scared."

"I might have."

"Travis...man, I could say a lot of things you already know. But only one of them really matters. That woman is our prime suspect."

"She's *your* prime suspect."

"And who's yours?"

"I'm not there yet."

After a moment's silence, Hank said, "Hey, buddy, you realize you're not acting like yourself, don't you? It's as if you met Celeste Langley and something short-circuited in your brain."

Ignoring that, he said, "Let's go."

Hank shook his head. "There's no point in both of us wasting our time with Reese."

He bit his tongue to keep from saying he didn't consider it a waste of time.

"So why don't I take care of some other stuff while you go talk to him. We can start in on the rest of the people on our Parker list later."

"Yeah. Why not. Good idea."

Travis turned and started away, unable to stop himself from thinking about what Hank had just said—and worrying that he was right.

Scientifically improbable as it might be, maybe meeting Celeste Langley really had short-circuited something in his brain.

What else would explain why he couldn't stop thinking about her for more than two seconds straight?

CHAPTER FOUR

Tuesday, October 5, 11:31 a.m.

EVAN REESE LIVED on the Upper East Side, in an apartment not far from Steve Parker's, which meant that by driving through Central Park Travis made the trip from Reese's to West Seventy-fourth in only a few minutes.

Even so, by the time he reached Celeste's block he'd told himself twelve dozen times that he shouldn't be going to her place. He could keep his promise to "get back to her" simply by phoning.

Of course, the problem with that was he wouldn't get to see her. And he wanted to—despite knowing it was a bad idea.

He shook his head, thinking how his sister was forever telling him that sooner or later he'd meet a woman who'd knock him off his feet. And that the longer it took, the harder he'd fall.

His response was always just to laugh, yet

now he was wondering if she'd been giving him a female version of Hank's short-circuit theory.

Maybe so. But regardless of anybody's theory, he knew that if he was smart he wouldn't go near Celeste again without Hank along. Not until they'd established who killed her brother.

After that, he could see as much of her as he liked. Assuming he was still interested. However, until then...

He *almost* managed to make himself drive straight past her building. He would have, except for the empty parking space directly across the street. In Manhattan, if that wasn't an omen he didn't know what would be.

He wheeled into it, cut the ignition and got out of the car—glancing up at her living room window, half expecting to see her standing there.

She wasn't, but she *was* home. And just the sound of her voice, when she responded to his buzz, was enough to make his pulse skip.

Telling himself he was here on police business, he started up the stairs to the third floor.

She was waiting for him in the doorway again, wearing a pale yellow sweater and jeans.

As absurd as it might be, the mere sight of her warmed him. Then she smiled and his temperature rose another couple of degrees.

"Hi," she said.

"Hi. I've been to see Evan Reese, so I figured I'd stop by for a minute."

"I'm glad you did."

As he passed her on his way into the apartment, he caught the faint scent of her perfume. It put him in mind of a sultry summer night—which did absolutely nothing to cool him down.

"Coffee?" she asked, gesturing him toward the living room.

"No, thanks. I won't stay long. I just wanted to tell you about Reese face-to-face, because…"

He paused, gathering his thoughts. There was a fine line between warning someone to be careful and scaring the wits out of her.

"Because?" she prompted.

"Because he told me it never even occurred to him that he'd make you nervous by calling. And that since he had, he wouldn't do it again. But I don't think you should count on it."

"Ah. And is he…should I be seriously worried about him?"

"It's hard to know. He lied when I asked why he'd told you we gave him your number. So we obviously can't believe anything he says."

"What was *his* story?"

"That he didn't say a word about how he'd gotten it."

"He *did*."

"I know. But that's not what he said this morning. He claimed he simply got it from Information."

"Did you tell him it's unlisted?"

"Uh-huh. He just shrugged and said they must have given it out by mistake."

"Is that possible?"

"It's very unlikely. And...look, he didn't mention anything about why he was seeing a psychiatrist. And I can't go rummaging through your brother's medical records without a search warrant, but..."

"Should you get one?" she asked quietly.

He'd love to. But it wasn't really an option.

"That's not as easy to do as TV makes it seem," he told her. "I'd need a good reason. One specifically related to the case, I mean. But even without knowing exactly what his problem is... Well, I think he's pretty unbalanced."

"Then I *should* be seriously worried."

"You should be seriously careful. If you notice anything suspicious... He's in his late thirties, short and slightly built, with dark hair and glasses. If anyone who fits that description shows up here or seems to be following you, phone me right away."

"Following me," she murmured.

"I'm not saying he will. I'm only saying it's possible he'll call again. Or try to see you. With any luck, though, you've heard the last of him."

Celeste slowly pushed her hair back from her face. "What about his saying he's a writer? Is he? Or was that just part of his *cosmic* gibberish?"

"It might be true. At least it's consistent with what he told Hank and me yesterday. He said his work's published in small, esoteric magazines."

"They don't pay much."

"No, we already thought of that. He probably tips the concierge in his building more at Christmas than that sort of writing would bring in. So whether he actually writes or not he must have another source of income. A trust fund or something was our best guess."

Celeste said nothing more, and as the silence grew Travis made himself say, "I've got to go. I just wanted to bring you up to speed."

"Thanks," she said, rising when he did. "I can't tell you how much I appreciate it. And...I did what you suggested and made the basic arrangements for Steve's service. But until I can tell them...I guess you still haven't heard when the autopsy will be?"

"No. I'll let you know as soon as I do."

"Thanks," she said again. Then she led the way to her door.

"I'll call you." He stepped out into the hallway. "Take care."

"I will," she promised, giving him a wan smile.

He started away, silently congratulating himself. He'd handled that pretty well for a guy with a short circuit in his brain.

After closing the door, Celeste watched through the peephole while Travis strode down the hall. Then, unable to resist the temptation this time around, she walked over to the living room window and stood waiting for him to appear on the street below.

When he did she felt a funny little flutter in her chest. She liked the man. Really liked him.

As he reached his car, he turned and looked up at her.

Her face suddenly felt warm. Then he raised his hand and smiled, making her a little less embarrassed about being caught watching.

Once he'd driven off she headed for her office, glad she had that deadline looming. It was forcing her to work, and even though she'd been having trouble concentrating, once she finally managed to lose herself in a manuscript she stopped thinking about other things.

Like her mother's accident. Or Steve's murder. Or the fact that her husband had been screwing around on her for who knew how long before she'd caught him at it. All in all, this hadn't been the best year of her life.

Telling herself dwelling on that would be a bad idea, she sat down at her desk. She hadn't even reached for her pencil when the phone rang.

The caller ID display was reading Caller Unknown, which made her hesitate about picking up. And as soon as she did, she wished she hadn't.

"This is Evan Reese," he announced.

A chill ran through her as she said, "Yes?"

"Why did you tell that cop I scared you?"

She thought rapidly, trying to remember precisely what Travis had said he'd told Reese. Something about his call making her "nervous." That was it.

"I didn't say you scared me," she said. "I only mentioned that you made me a little nervous."

"Sure you did."

She swallowed uneasily, suddenly suspecting that what Travis had said to her wasn't quite what he'd said to Reese.

"I don't really recall the exact words I used. But maybe I said you made me kind of anxious. I'm not used to strangers phoning and—"

"Kind of anxious? If that's all you told him, then the guy's a wacko. Listen, Celeste, I didn't like the way he talked to me this morning. And I didn't like the way he went racing to your place afterward, either."

He'd followed Travis here! The cordless still to her ear, she pushed back her chair.

"So you tell him that, huh? Tell him I'm wise to his tricks and I don't like them."

"Yes, I will," she said, hurrying out of her office.

"Don't forget. And tell him he hasn't heard the last about his visit here. Tell him I've got friends in high places, and he's going to be very sorry he tried to lean on me."

"I'll tell him."

As she reached the living room window, Snoops scurried down off the window seat and ran to hide, clearly sensing her fear.

Cautiously, she peeked out. No one was standing on the street, but the man could be hiding just out of sight. Or maybe he'd even gotten into her building. That thought sent a fresh ripple of anxiety through her.

"Are you still there?" Reese demanded.

"Yes," she said. "But I'm afraid I have to go now. Someone's at my door."

Without another word, she broke the connection. Then she took a few deep breaths, trying to stop her heart from pounding. After it had slowed to somewhere near normal, she pressed in Travis's number.

CELESTE SOUNDED as if she was terrified but was doing her utmost to hide it, and each word she spoke made Travis feel more like killing Evan Reese.

"Want me to head back to your place?" he asked when she'd finished.

She hesitated, the silence lasting long enough to tell him she did.

Just as he was about to make a U-turn, she said, "No. Thanks, but I'll be fine once I calm down. And I'm sure holding my hand isn't in your job description."

That was true, although the thought of doing so was far more appealing than anything that *was* in his job description.

"But what about you?" she asked. "He really seemed intent on causing trouble."

"Let him try. The C.O.'s used to complaints. But, look, is your phone a cordless?"

"Yes."

"Then take it with you into the hall. Make sure he isn't there. Check the staircase, too. I'll hold on."

"All right."

While he listened to the faint clicks of her locks turning he had a horrible vision—her discovering that Reese was standing just beyond where she'd have been able to see him through the peephole.

"All clear?" he demanded at the sound of the door opening.

"Seems to be."

The vision took so long to fade that he almost told her to forget about the staircase. Then he stopped himself. If Reese *had* gotten into the building, better she discovered it now than later.

His chest strangely tight, he imagined her walking down the hall, its carpet swallowing the whispers of her footsteps. She should be about reaching the stairs and—

The stairway door creaked faintly.

"I still don't see him," she said.

"Good." Of course, that didn't guarantee he wasn't there someplace. However, her cordless couldn't have much more range, so going further wouldn't be safe.

"Should I head back to my apartment?"

"Yeah. He's probably home by now. But if anything else worries you, just call."

"Thanks," she murmured.

He began picturing her again—with her brilliant blue and eyes and pretty smile. It was enough to make him reconsider the idea of going straight back over there.

"I'm just locking my door," she said after a few moments.

"Okay. I'll check in with you later."

"Thanks, but you don't have to."

"Following up *is* in my job description."

"Ah. Well…I wouldn't want you not doing your job."

Her tone made him suspect she was smiling, although that might only be wishful thinking.

"Talk to you later, then. Bye."

"Bye, Travis."

After pressing the End button he began thinking about paying Evan Reese yet another visit. However, that wouldn't be a wise move. He was too mad to face the guy.

Besides, leaning on him obviously hadn't helped matters. Instead of scaring him off Celeste, it had only made things worse.

He was still mentally kicking himself about that when he reached Manhattan North Homicide. And it didn't improve his mood to find that Hank wasn't there, ready and willing to discuss the situation.

According to the other detectives in the squad room, he'd left shortly after Travis had headed for Reese's place.

After fishing out his phone, he was about to press the speed dial for Hank's number when Len Espizito, C.O. of Homicide, materialized.

"My office, Quinn," he said, turning on his heel.

Travis stuck the phone back in his pocket and followed the lieutenant, wondering what was up.

It didn't even occur to him that the problem was Evan Reese until Espizito shoved his door shut behind them and said, "Okay, let's hear *your* version of the visit you paid this Reese character."

"You mean the one yesterday or the one this morning?" he asked, buying himself a few seconds to think.

"Which do you figure I mean?" Espizito snapped. "The guy phoned me ten minutes ago, screaming police brutality."

"What? I didn't touch him."

"Maybe not, but did you threaten to?"

"I told him to leave Parker's sister alone. That was basically it."

"Then you headed directly to the sister's apartment? On your own?"

He shrugged, glad he'd already known that Reese had followed him. Otherwise, Espizito would have caught him even more off guard.

"Did you?" he demanded.

"Yes."

"And Reese says you were at her place last night. And that since it was after he called her it had to have been late."

Crap. Instead of implying he'd merely talked to Celeste on the phone, he'd specifically told Reese he'd gone there. As a way of emphasizing how upset she'd been. But it looked as if he shouldn't have gotten specific.

"Is that true? Were you there alone with her last night, too?"

"Lieutenant, the guy had called and scared her. Hank was already on his way home, and I just wanted to—"

"Don't give me any crap, Quinn. Reese said it's obvious you like her. Do you?"

Travis mentally kicked himself once more. His partner realizing he found Celeste attractive was one thing. But it must be written all over him for a stranger to have picked up on it.

"Do you?" Espizito repeated.

"No. She seems like a nice woman, that's all."

"Ballantyne was in earlier. And I asked him about the Parker case. According to your own partner, this *nice woman*—who, by the way, he mentioned is a looker—could be our killer."

"She isn't."

"No? You're sure of that? Even though Ballantyne isn't?"

"Sir, there was a blond woman in the hall outside Parker's apartment the night he was killed and Celeste Langley is blond. Along with a few million other women in the city. Hank just doesn't like to rule anyone out too fast."

The C.O. shot him a skeptical glance, but all he said was "Regardless of that, this has bad news written all over it. Your being in an attractive female suspect's apartment. Alone with her. Repeatedly."

"Twice is hardly repeatedly. And I only—"

"I don't care if you're as innocent as a day-old baby. You know the drill. We avoid situations that could appear compromising. And consider the mileage someone intent on causing you trouble might get out of this. Do you want Internal Affairs climbing all over you? Because that's where it could go."

"I—"

"Quinn, you have no idea who Evan Reese is."

"Sure I do. He's a nut bar."

"Could be. But does the name Fred Corstair ring a bell?"

"Of course." Corstair was the first deputy police commissioner. Which made him the most powerful civilian affiliated with the department.

"Good. Then consider this. Evan Reese's mother is Corstair's sister. Reese laid that on me when he phoned and I just finished checking it out."

"What?"

"Yup," Espizito muttered. "Your nut bar is extremely well connected. His uncle Fred can pull just about any strings he feels like around here. And if I don't 'set you straight,' as Reese put it, he'll be on the phone to Corstair."

The C.O. paused. When Travis remained silent, he added, "In case you haven't heard, I'm already in *Uncle Fred's* bad books."

"I've heard."

Barely a week ago, a team of Manhattan North Homicide detectives had wrapped up a particularly gruesome case—by charging the wrong man.

Two days later, the real killer's lawyer convinced him to confess. And when the charges against the innocent suspect were dropped, he announced that he intended to sue the department.

The media had had a field day with the story, and Fred Corstair appeared to be holding Len Espizito personally responsible. For the false arrest, the resulting bad press *and* the pending lawsuit.

"By setting you straight," Espizito was saying, "Reese means he wants you off the Parker case. Claims your involvement with the vic's sister is totally unprofessional and—"

"I'm *not* involved with her!"

"Fine, you're not. But that's how he's painting it. There's also his claim that you threatened him with bodily harm. And he says he's sure you'll continue to harass him if I leave you on the case."

"He'll calm down."

Espizito shook his head. "If I don't do something to mollify him, he'll be pushing for your shield."

"Lieutenant…I'm sorry I've put you in this position. But I know you don't give in to threats."

"No. Not normally. Only, this time it seems like the smartest option. The last thing I need right now is a loose cannon with connections to Corstair."

"But—"

"No," the C.O. said again. "Look, let's say I tell Reese I've given you a verbal reprimand and that's as far as I'm taking it. What do you think he'll do?

"He'll talk to Uncle Fred, just like he threatened," Espizito continued before Travis could open his mouth. "Then Corstair will be on Internal Affairs. And on me for good measure. So I'm going to avoid a whole lot of grief for both of us.

"I'm assigning Koscina to work with Ballantyne as the other primary on this one. And I want you to take some time off. You've got a pile of overtime built up. I've already had a memo from personnel about it, so—"

"You can't do this!"

"No? Watch me."

"Sir...I really want to stay on the case."

Espizito opened his office door and said, "Sorry, Quinn. Two weeks' leave. Starting now. End of discussion."

CHAPTER FIVE

Tuesday, October 5, 1:09 p.m.

JUST AS TRAVIS was driving out of the precinct parking garage, he spotted his partner's red Jeep heading toward it.

"Had lunch yet?" Hank said, pulling up beside the Mustang.

"Uh-uh."

"Good. Me, neither. I'll just park and we can go grab something."

"Let's take both cars."

"Well...sure, if you want. Lucy's?"

He nodded, then started off again. His stomach felt like solid concrete, so the last thing he needed was food. But he'd talk while Hank ate. Maybe, between the two of them, they could figure out a way of convincing Espizito to put him back on the case.

In Lucy's, Hank ordered the daily special. When Travis told the waitress he only wanted coffee, Hank gave him a curious look.

"You sick?" he asked as the woman turned away.

"No. But Espizito just yanked me off the Parker case."

"He what?"

Quickly, Travis filled in the details.

Once he was done, Hank sat looking lost in thought. Finally, he said, "You know, buddy, you're not going to like me telling you this, but maybe it's for the best."

"Why?"

"Because, since the first moment you laid eyes on Celeste Langley... But we've already been over that. Besides, there's something new.

"Remember the other night? When we were talking about the coincidence of her mother and brother dying within such a brief time span? I said I wanted to know whether she had anything to gain from their deaths."

Travis nodded, aware of the icy numbness at the base of his spine.

"Well, she did. While you were visiting Reese I went over to probate. Had a look at Adele Langley's will."

"And?"

"And, first off, she seems to have left a

pretty substantial estate. Which she bequeathed entirely to her two children—half to Parker, half to Celeste."

"Nothing surprising about that."

"No. But there's a survivor clause. If either beneficiary fails to survive the mother by ninety days, the entire estate goes to the remaining one. And Parker was murdered just short of the ninety days."

"That doesn't mean Celeste killed him," Travis said, trying to ignore the numbness creeping up his backbone.

"No," Hank agreed slowly. "But the will would have been read shortly after Adele Langley's death. So even if Celeste didn't know the terms until then, there's been a lot of time for her to think about... Well, you know what I'm saying."

In the three years he'd worked with Hank, Travis had rarely been angry with him. Right now, though, he was so mad the only smart thing to do was keep his mouth shut.

Leaning forward, Hank clasped his hands on the table between them. "Buddy, I know you don't want to believe she did it, but so far she's our only real suspect and—"

"Exactly," he interrupted as calmly as he

could. "*So far.* The investigation's barely under way. We haven't looked an inch beyond her. And what would her motive have been? You really figure that when she's already getting half of a 'substantial estate' she'd kill her own brother for the other half? Exactly how much are we talking, anyway?"

"Impossible to tell, just from the will. It's written in terms of assets, not amounts. But, among other things, it mentions a stock portfolio and investment certificates. So it could be fairly serious money."

"Even so, do you really think she'd murder her brother to get her hands on his share? Did you honestly read her that way?"

Hank shrugged. "What you see isn't always what you get. Could be she's greedy. Or in debt up to her eyeballs. I doubt editors make bags of money, and she had some awfully nice stuff in her apartment."

"Which could well have been her mother's. If the woman left a substantial estate, it's only logical that she had nice stuff. Hank, you're reaching so far on this…"

"Maybe I am," he said quietly. "Or maybe she had a motive other than money."

"Or maybe someone else killed Parker.

Someone with a motive that had nothing to do with Adele Langley's will. Let's not forget that possibility, huh?"

"I'm not. I'm only... Look, Travis, I'd never say a negative word about you. That's a given, right? I'd never have gone to Espizito and told him I figured you might be less than objective on this one. But, as I said, maybe his yanking you is for the best. So why don't you just roll with it."

Travis exhaled slowly. His partner obviously didn't want to go to bat for him with the lieutenant. Which meant there was no way in the world he'd get back on the case.

"Why not take off somewhere for a couple of weeks," Hank suggested. "Go lie on a beach down south and completely forget about the job."

Even though he stopped there, Travis knew he was dying to add *And completely forget about Celeste Langley.*

He stared at the table for a minute, then focused on Hank once more. "You know I'm not the lying-on-the-beach type, so I'll probably just stick around the city. And do me a favor?"

"Sure."

"Keep me up-to-date? Stay in touch and let me know what you're finding?"

Hank hesitated for a second, then nodded.

"And don't go getting tunnel vision."

"I don't intend to."

"You'll check out Jill Flores's alibi?"

"You know I will."

"And talk to Evan Reese again, huh?"

"Why?"

Travis shrugged. "I can't stop wondering about him phoning Celeste last night, let alone again this morning. Why bother calling her to say he's pissed off at me? Why didn't he just call Espizito straightaway? I keep thinking it's a classic example of the perp trying to involve himself in the case as much as possible."

"Travis—"

"Don't look so skeptical. You know that happens. And the odds on it go way up when the killer's a loony-tune."

Hank frowned.

"Being Corstair's nephew doesn't mean he can't be a murderer."

"Yeah," Hank finally muttered. "You're right."

"And be sure you—"

"Travis, give it a rest, okay? We've worked together long enough that you know I'll follow up on *all* the angles."

"Yeah, I know. But make sure that's Koscina's attitude, too, huh? 'Cuz I'm still convinced Celeste didn't have a thing to do with Parker's death."

TRAVIS PACED his living room, considering the situation one more time.

Like it or not, and he definitely didn't like it, he was off the Parker case and on leave from the department. However, he was still a cop. So, as Espizito had reminded him only a couple of hours ago, he was supposed to avoid situations that might appear compromising.

Logic, then, said that since he knew Celeste was a suspect in her brother's murder he should stay completely away from her. On the other hand, he'd made it clear to both Hank and Espizito that *he* didn't suspect her.

Adding that factor into the equation, what was the worst-case scenario?

He didn't stay away and got his knuckles rapped if Espizito found out. Possibly rapped pretty hard.

But how would Espizito find out?

In all likelihood, he wouldn't, which pretty much eliminated the need for concern.

Of course, there was the *other* worst-case scenario. The one he didn't want to even think about but was making himself. What if Celeste *had* killed her brother?

He still didn't really figure there was a chance she had, but his gut instincts about people weren't one hundred percent accurate. Besides, he couldn't call himself a detective and simply ignore that survivor clause.

It *did* give Celeste an obvious motive. And if she had no one to substantiate her alibi for Saturday evening... But maybe she did. Maybe someone had phoned her and they'd had a lengthy conversation.

He reminded himself the estimated time of death was between nine and midnight. Which meant it would have had to be a pretty long conversation to let her entirely off the hook. Still, it was worth asking her about. And he could also... No. He couldn't.

He couldn't ask her anything that would lead to a discussion of how Hank and Koscina might build a case against her. If he did that and it ever came out, he'd find himself back walking a beat. Or off the force entirely.

That was such a grim thought, it started Hank's words drifting through his head once more. *Why not take off somewhere for a couple of weeks. Go lie on a beach down south and completely forget about the job.*

Maybe that was what he *should* do. But if he did, who'd be looking out for Celeste while he was gone? Who'd follow up if Evan Reese scared the wits out of her again? Or worse?

He shook his head, thinking there was little doubt about the outcome of this mental discussion with himself. So he might as well just give it up and go see her.

There was no way he could simply forget all about the case simply because he was officially off it. Or forget all about her. And no way he'd be satisfied until he knew who'd killed Parker.

What if you end up learning it was Celeste? asked the voice in his head that sounded exactly like Hank's.

If I get any evidence of that, I'll turn it over to you, partner, he silently replied. *So you can throw her in the slammer.*

Telling himself there wasn't a chance in a million that would be the end result, he grabbed his keys and headed downstairs.

He'd left his car parked down the block, near Ninth, and he started rapidly along West Twenty-eighth in that direction.

Out front of the building next to his, a couple of local punks were in the midst of a shoving match that looked as if it might escalate. He thought about stopping and having a little chat with them, but decided not to waste his breath.

Just beyond them, an old guy was picking through a trash can. A few yards farther along, a bag lady was loudly berating a parked Jeep about something.

Home sweet home. And Chelsea was one of the better neighborhoods in Lower Manhattan.

He reached the Mustang and climbed in. Barely fifteen minutes later, he was at the front door of Celeste's building, buzzing her apartment.

"Yes?" she said, sounding nervous.

"It's Travis."

"Oh."

Sounding pleased, he thought, smiling. If he'd had the slightest lingering doubt about coming here, it had just vanished.

As she released the lock he opened the

door, then hurried up the stairs. Walking out of the stairwell was a déjà vu experience.

He saw her waiting in her doorway and suddenly felt warm inside. Her welcoming smile made him warmer still.

"When you said you'd 'check in,' I assumed that just meant you'd call," she said, gesturing him into the apartment.

"Well, something's come up that I wanted to talk to you about in person."

"Oh?"

"It'll take a few minutes."

"Then we'd better go sit down." She turned and started toward the living room.

He glanced at the hall closet before he followed along, wondering whether there was a gray trench coat in it. He wasn't going to ask, though.

And even if there was, it wouldn't mean much. As he'd told Hank, half the women in New York had gray trench coats.

In the living room, Celeste simply eyed him until he said, "Okay, here's what's happened. I'm no longer assigned to your brother's case. In fact, I'm on leave for the next couple of weeks."

Her blue eyes filled with uncertainty. "Why?"

"That doesn't really matter."

"It was Evan Reese, wasn't it? He *did* call and complain about you."

"Uh-huh, that was mostly what did it."

"Oh, no," she whispered. "I should never have phoned you about him. I—"

"Yes, you should have. This isn't your fault. Or mine, really. I was only doing my job by talking to him." He shrugged. "I guess I just came on too strong."

"But…that sort of thing can't look good on your record."

"It isn't anything much. Officially, I'm just using up overtime. And my being off the case won't affect the end result. Whether I'm working it or not, they'll find the killer.

"You're sure?"

He nodded. "It's not as if only Hank and I were assigned to it. We were just the primaries. He has an entire squad of detectives he can call on, and when a case is fresh we always devote a lot of manpower to it. So… well, as I said, they'll find the killer."

"I hope so. I can't imagine never knowing who… Left forever wondering."

"I know. People sometimes ask why I'd choose to work in Homicide. But that's one of the positive things. Helping the victims' families."

He hesitated then, trying to decide whether he should actually risk taking this any further—reminding himself that if he did and it turned out he was reading Celeste wrong, he could end up in major trouble.

On the other hand, Hank was a master at blindsiding suspects. And the thought of Celeste not even realizing she had a problem until someone was reading her her rights...

He felt as if he were about to step onto a tightrope without a safety net. But as long as he was careful about what he said and didn't tell her anything she didn't already know, he wouldn't *really* be doing anything he shouldn't.

"Look...Celeste," he began. "I'm trusting you won't repeat what I'm about to say."

"All right," she agreed slowly.

He hesitated once more, then said, "Remember, when Hank and I were here on Sunday, he mentioned that your brother might have had a female visitor shortly before he was killed?"

"Yes. But I wasn't thinking straight at the time. I explained that, didn't I? Told you it was hours before I realized I should have said it was probably Jill Flores?"

"Uh-huh. You told me."

"And?" she prompted when he didn't continue right away.

"And...do you remember him asking if you were in your brother's apartment that night?"

"Yes. I said I wasn't. That I was right here, working."

He nodded.

For a moment she merely looked confused, then she murmured, "Oh, no. Travis, are you saying he thinks..."

She shook her head, as if finding the realization impossible to comprehend. "Are you saying he thinks *I* might have killed Steve?" she asked at last. "And...what about you? Do *you* think—"

"No. I don't."

When she caught her bottom lip with her teeth he had an almost uncontrollable urge to move nearer and wrap his arms around her.

Instead, he made himself stay right where he was and said, "Celeste...this is a tricky situation. I can't really discuss the specifics of the case with you, but...let me talk in generalities, okay?"

"Okay," she said, gazing at him.

Her eyes were a darker blue than usual—colored, he knew, by fear. And her skin had grown pale.

He gave her a reassuring smile before saying, "I know you've heard this a million times on TV, but I just want you to think about it for a minute.

"Until a suspect has been read her rights, nothing she says to a police officer can be used in a court of law. But once she *is* read her rights, it's in her best interest not to say another word until she has a lawyer present."

Hesitating one more time, he assured himself there was no such charge as "counseling a suspect." Then he added, "And someone in a...potentially uncomfortable position might want to talk to a good criminal lawyer. Get a clear understanding of where she stands."

"You're saying I'm a *serious* suspect," she whispered.

"I'm speaking in general terms," he said, hoping his expression was telling her that was only because he had no choice. "But if anyone asked me to recommend a good criminal lawyer, I certainly could."

"Oh, Travis," she murmured. "This can't be happening."

He gazed at her for a long moment, aware that getting involved with her would only be begging for trouble. But she was so clearly distraught that he couldn't stop himself from sliding along the couch and taking her in his arms.

"Oh, Travis," she murmured again.

CELESTE RESTED her cheek against the solid warmth of Travis's shoulder, acutely aware she hadn't been held like this in a long, long time.

It felt good to have someone care. To have this *particular* someone care. This man whose scent started her thinking about autumn in the country.

She wished she could simply drink in his strength and pretend everything was wonderful in her little corner of the world. But she was nowhere near that good at pretense.

Detective Hank Ballantyne suspected her of murdering Steve. So even though Travis didn't… Or was he only claiming he didn't?

An unsettled feeling began snaking through her as she considered that.

NYPD detectives were a devious bunch. Her estranged husband must have told her a hundred different stories about sneaky things they did.

Not that Bryce had heard the stories first-hand. He was an estate lawyer, had nothing to do with the police. But the criminal lawyers in his firm would talk and...

And what if Travis Quinn's "concern" was nothing but an act to make her trust him? So she'd confess to the killing?

What if he wasn't actually off the case at all? If he'd merely told her that as part of a ruse?

She eased out of his arms, the thought that he might be trying to trick her making her cold all over.

"It's going to be okay," he said softly.

"Not if I get charged with murder it isn't. Travis, I didn't do it."

"I know."

"Then why does your partner think I did?"

"He only figures it's a possibility."

"But why? Because Steve had a female visitor on Saturday night and I was home alone? With no one to vouch for the fact? What kind of evidence is that? Doesn't he need a motive? Some reason I'd have wanted to—"

"Look...I just can't go into the whys. I—"

"Oh," she whispered, suddenly realizing what must have happened. "You know about the survivor clause in my mother's will, don't you? That's it, isn't it?" she added when Travis didn't say a word.

"But how could Hank think I'm the kind of person who'd—"

"Celeste, when you're a detective..." He paused, shaking his head. "I can't go into the whys," he said again. "I was bending the rules by saying anything at all. Maybe I *shouldn't* have said anything.

"It was just...well, I decided you had to know in advance that you might have a problem. On the off chance it materializes."

Was that the truth? Had he simply wanted to warn her? Exhaling slowly, she recalled what he'd said about rights.

Until a suspect has been read her rights, nothing she says to a police officer can be used in a court of law.

Didn't that mean he *couldn't* be trying to trick her? Because even if she confessed, he wouldn't be able to use... But he'd know for sure that she was guilty. And all he'd have left to do was come up with proof.

Of course, there wasn't any. Because she hadn't killed Steve.

Sometimes, though, innocent people got railroaded.

She gazed uncertainly at Travis, her intuition telling her he was on her side but her brain warning her not to risk making a dreadful mistake.

"I'll be back in a sec," she said at last, pushing herself up from the couch and heading for her office.

CHAPTER SIX

Tuesday, October 5, 4:12 p.m.

CELESTE FIRMLY CLOSED her office door, then grabbed her cordless and the card Travis had given her. Along with his cellular number, there was an office number on it. She punched that one in, then held her breath.

"Manhattan North Homicide," a man answered. "Detective Ovner speaking."

"Detective Quinn, please."

"Sorry, he's not here. Can someone else help you?"

"No, I need to talk to him. Do you know when he'll be there?"

"Just a minute. I'll check."

She waited, her heart beating fast, until Ovner picked up again.

"Detective Quinn's on leave for a couple of weeks."

"Oh."

"You sure no one else can help you?"

"No. Thanks, but it's not urgent."

Just as she clicked the phone off, she realized the call hadn't actually gotten her anywhere.

If Travis had come up with a devious master plot, he was smart enough to have covered all the bases. He wouldn't have left things so she could trip him up with a simple phone call. But there had to be *some* way of determining where he really stood.

Closing her eyes, she began to systematically review everything he'd said from the moment he'd arrived. When she got to his suggestion about talking to a lawyer she felt as if a light had just been switched on inside her head.

An attorney who intentionally violated lawyer-client privilege would be risking disbarment. So even though Travis had offered to recommend someone, he couldn't possibly have been hoping the lawyer would repeat anything she said. In fact, if he was trying to set her up, the last thing he'd want was her getting legal advice—whether it was from someone he knew or a stranger.

She carefully thought through her reasoning a second time, afraid she'd find it was faulty. But it still made perfect sense, which meant that she could trust Travis Quinn.

"That's a relief," she whispered.

Knowing that he really had to be on her side didn't make her problem go away, but it made her feel immeasurably better. It also gave her a serious twinge of guilt about suspecting him of plotting against her.

Telling herself it was only prudent not to trust someone until you were sure you could, she headed back to the living room—where Snoops was now perched on the far end of the couch from Travis, staring at him.

"She doesn't seem too sure about me," he said.

"She's a he. Or maybe I should say an it. Whatever, you should be flattered. He normally hides from company."

Picking up the cat, she sat down with him on her lap.

"Everything okay now?" Travis asked quietly.

"'Okay's' pushing it, but I've recovered from my initial shock."

"Good."

Assuring herself once more that she could trust him, she said, "When you mentioned criminal lawyers? You really think I should talk to one?"

"Uh-huh. Just to be on the safe side. So that if the guys do decide to bring you in for questioning there's someone who already knows the basic story. And knows you."

"All right. Then I'll do it."

"Would you like a couple of names?"

"You won't get in trouble for giving them to me?"

"Not as long as nobody finds out," he told her, scrolling through his phone.

"They won't find out from me."

He smiled briefly, then said, "Celeste, this is going to end up just fine. Even if they officially question you, that's a world away from charging you. And we simply don't charge the wrong people with homicides."

"Never? Wasn't there something in the news, only a week or two ago…?"

"Yeah…well…it *almost* never happens. And it won't happen to you."

She nodded, although if he was *certain* of that, would he be advising her to see a lawyer?

Forcing the question from her mind, she went to get the cordless out of her office.

The first man she called was upstate, in the

midst of a trial. The second one's assistant informed her that he just couldn't fit any new clients into his schedule at present.

Celeste almost mentioned Travis's name, thinking it might help, but stopped herself in time. If they didn't want the wrong people learning that he was behind her getting legal advice she'd better be careful what she said.

"You know the old saying," he told her as she punched in the last number he'd given her. "Third time lucky."

She dearly hoped the old saying was right, because it was almost five o'clock.

When Walter Namouth's secretary said it would be the end of next week before Celeste could see him, she decided things were getting desperate. So, as much as she hated associating herself with Bryce, she gave it a shot.

"I'm sorry, but I forgot I was supposed to tell you that my husband, Bryce Wayland, spoke to Mr. Namouth about seeing me. Bryce is an attorney with Price, Whitechurch and Hoskins, and...well the thing is that Mr. Namouth assured Bryce he'd fit me in as soon as possible. I'm afraid the problem's urgent."

"Oh. He didn't mention anything to me, but...let's see...I could probably squeeze you in tomorrow morning."

"That would be wonderful."

"Fine. Ten o'clock?"

"Perfect. Thank you."

Clicking off, she said to Travis, "Ten o'clock tomorrow. The only problem is that if she repeats our conversation to Namouth they might throw me out on my ear. I'll bet he's never even heard of Bryce."

"But Bryce is actually a lawyer?"

"Yes."

"Then I guess you could have gotten him to recommend someone."

"No, I wouldn't ask him for help."

After a few moments of silence, Travis said, "The other night you mentioned that you left him. If I asked why, would you tell me it's none of my business?"

She shook her head, thinking she was so grateful to him that she'd answer just about any question he asked.

"He had a girlfriend," she explained, surprised to discover it no longer hurt to say the words. "An off-Broadway actress named Donna Rainfield. And I found out about her."

"Some guys are idiots," Travis said quietly. "And I don't mean for letting you find out."

"Yes...well...it hurt a lot at first. He tried to convince me she didn't mean anything to him, that it had been a mistake and would never happen again, but I knew deep down it would. We...

"Bryce isn't really an awful person. When my mother died he offered to do whatever he could to help. And he called me yesterday, about Steve—again, saying that if I needed anything all I had to do was let him know.

"So it's not as if he's the Devil incarnate. We just shouldn't have ended up together.

"If we'd taken things more slowly, gotten to know each other better, I doubt we would have. But...well, after the initial glow wore off it wasn't the marriage of the century. Not by any means and...the truth is that he hurt my pride as much as my heart."

She hesitated, then decided she might as well finish the story. "A few days after I moved out Donna moved in. So much for her having meant nothing to him."

CELESTE SPRINKLED more cheese on her spaghetti, then snuck a glance across the table at Travis.

She was glad he'd stayed, because otherwise she'd be dwelling, utterly and exclusively, on her problem. Whereas with him here, while she'd made dinner he'd talked about what a brilliant lawyer Walter Namouth was—which had started her believing that things weren't nearly as bad as they might have been.

Surely, between Namouth's brilliance and the fact she was innocent, there was no possible way she'd end up charged with murder.

"Terrific garlic bread," Travis said, reaching for another slice.

"Glad you like it." She let her gaze linger on him a little longer this time. She wasn't entirely certain what had prompted her to invite him to stay, but...

Oh, who was she trying to fool? She liked him.

Merely focusing on those laugh lines around his eyes was enough to make her smile, and she loved the way his square-cut jaw proclaimed he was a tough guy, while his quiet manner of speaking said not *too* tough. And his country-autumn scent was so enticing that she actually found herself breathing more deeply when she was near him.

Most of all, though, she liked the way he'd taken her in his arms to comfort her when she'd been upset. Until those stupid suspicions had begun tiptoeing around in her head, his holding her had felt perfectly right.

But regardless of that, the last thing she intended to do was get carried away.

As she'd reminded herself before, her life had been a series of upheavals this past year. And she knew enough psychology to realize she should be treading very carefully when it came to anything involving her emotions.

Even at the best of times, peoples' feelings for one another could change. What seemed perfectly right, here and now, might feel completely different a few months or years down the road. She'd learned her lesson on that score, and was never going to repeat her mistake.

Of course, Travis was nothing like Bryce. Still, she wasn't about to rush into another relationship. Especially not when she suspected that she and Travis didn't really have a lot in common.

Under normal circumstances, their paths would never even have crossed. She'd only met him because he was a cop doing his job and...

But did that really matter? It was the man behind the badge she was falling for.

Falling for. As the words echoed in her mind, she told herself that trying to deny them would be pointless. Her attraction to him was very rapidly developing into something more.

The question was, how should she handle that? She was going to have to do some serious thinking about—

"Dinner was great," Travis said. "I've always thought my mother makes the best spaghetti and meatballs outside of Italy, but now I'm not so sure."

His smile started a funny little fluttering around her heart.

"You should see what I can do when it's not a spur-of-the-moment invitation," she teased.

"I'd love to."

When he caught her gaze there was warmth in his eyes.

Searching for something to say that would stop him watching her, she settled on, "You know, you've never mentioned anything about your family before. I guess we've been so focused on all the bad stuff... But tell me a bit."

"Well, let's see. I've got a mother, a father, a sister who's three years younger than me, a niece who's two and another on the way.

"Actually, we don't know whether it's a girl, but it's definitely on the way. Then there's the regular assortment of other relatives."

"And...? You could give me a *few* more details."

When he smiled again, the funny little flutter returned.

"Okay. My parents live in Queens, which is where I grew up. My sister, Denise, and her family live on Staten Island. My father has his own business—basically manages some small apartment buildings. My mother was a teacher, but she retired a few years ago. Can I stop yet?"

She laughed. "Yes, that's probably all I can absorb at once.

"Besides," she added, pushing back her chair, "as glad as I am that you could stay, I've got to throw you out now. I promised to have a manuscript ready for pickup tomorrow afternoon, and that appointment with Namouth means I'll have to finish working on it tonight."

"You seem to spend a lot of evenings working."

"I think there's a special rule for the self-employed. Usually, you're either in the midst of a dry spell or swamped."

"And right now you're swamped?"

"No, right now I'm just pressed for time on this manuscript."

"Then we could do dinner again tomorrow. My treat."

She hesitated, wondering if, by then, she'd have had enough thinking time. "Well...yes," she finally said. "That would be nice."

"Good. I'll come by around seven, okay?"

"Fine."

When she walked him to the door, he simply gave her another warm smile and said, "See you tomorrow."

"Right. Around seven." She locked up behind him, then once again wandered over to the front window so she could see him when he appeared on the street below.

As she waited, her thoughts returned to the subject of what was happening between them. *Why* was she so drawn to this particular man at this particular time?

Was it a straightforward, Cupid-shot-an-arrow sort of attraction? Or was it something a whole lot more complex?

She'd pretty well come to terms with her marriage breaking up, but her mother's death was still giving her a lot of sleepless nights. And now Steve had been murdered and she was a suspect.

Man, if anyone could use an emotional anchor it was her. So was that what Travis represented to her subconscious?

It could well be. The fact that he was a cop, an authority figure… The way he'd come riding along like the proverbial white knight, doing battle for her with Evan Reese… And, most important, he believed in her innocence despite his partner's suspicions.

She stood looking down at him as he walked out of the building and headed across to his car. When he reached it, he turned and raised his hand the way he'd done earlier.

This time, she didn't feel embarrassed. This time, she smiled and raised hers in return.

HE'D BEEN ROAMING West Seventy-fourth, getting a sense of how many people were on this block of it in the evening.

Very few, it turned out. And that had started him thinking that if he *did* end up having to whack the Langley woman in her apartment, then coming to do the job under the cover of darkness would be a good idea.

It was about then that he'd spotted her staring down at the street.

For a moment he'd imagined her in his gun site. Centered in the window, a perfect target.

One shot, instant death. But when the time came he wouldn't be standing around waiting for her to show her face at a window.

Curious about why she was looking out, he'd stepped into the sheltering shadow of a staircase and watched the scene unfold.

The dark-haired man coming out of the building. Crossing to the black Mustang. Turning to gaze up at Celeste Langley. Her smiling.

Even from a hundred feet away the Ice Man thought he could smell a cop—which started him swearing under his breath.

When he'd checked her out he'd figured there'd be no problems at all. A woman on her own was easy prey. All he'd have to do was wait for the go-ahead, then make his move. But if the cop was her boyfriend there could be complications.

The Mustang had started to pull away from the curb, so he memorized the plate number. It was no big deal to get an ownership run, and he would. But he was almost certain the guy was heat. Had a sixth sense about that. And if he was right he'd priced the job too cheaply.

He shook his head, wishing he hadn't already taken the money. But he had, so he was committed.

In his business, when you agreed to do a job you did it. Otherwise, the word hit the street and your rep hit the skids.

When he looked back at the window, Celeste Langley was gone. That didn't matter, though. He'd already seen enough to know he'd have to be careful.

In fact, he'd better come by again tomorrow night. See if this guy was here all the time.

AT A QUARTER PAST TEN the next morning, Travis pulled into an empty parking space near the renovated SoHo building that housed Walter Namouth's office. He climbed out of his car and headed through the dazzling October sunshine in the direction of the front door.

He didn't intend to go inside. Not even into the lobby. But he wanted to talk to Celeste after she'd finished with the lawyer.

As promised, Hank was unofficially keeping him informed. He'd called last night to say that Steve Parker's autopsy was scheduled for today. And since that wasn't the sort of thing you told a dead man's sister over the phone, coming by to wait for Celeste made sense.

This way, he could drive her home, hear what Namouth had had to say and see how she was feeling about things at this point.

He'd pretty well figured out how he was feeling about them. His brain had refused to shut down and let him sleep last night, so he'd spent a lot of time thinking. And he'd reached some conclusions about just how helpful he could be to Celeste—without doing anything that would put Espizito into cardiac arrest if he heard about it.

Accompanying her to a meeting with a criminal lawyer would definitely not have been a wise move. Neither would letting her in on anything Hank told him about what was happening with the case.

But the department didn't own him. Besides, he was on leave, which meant that what he did with his time really wasn't anyone's business except his own.

As he reached the front of the building he was telling himself that if one of his friends had a problem and came to him for advice, he wouldn't hesitate to give it. Or if one of them just wanted someone to talk to, he'd listen. And Celeste was fast becoming a friend. Oh, maybe not exactly a friend, but...

Well, the terminology didn't matter. What mattered was that there was no reason he couldn't be there for her.

None except the minor detail that she was a suspect. Still, it wouldn't take Hank long to realize he had that one wrong.

Of course, if he didn't... Man, if he didn't, then Celeste would *really* need a friend.

Travis walked on past the building and down the block a few hundred feet, trying not to think he might have let a flaw or two creep into his logic. Because regardless of that possibility he wanted to spend as much time with her as she'd let him.

Maybe he hadn't known her long, but he was already reconsidering his theory about cops and serious relationships. They weren't *always* a bad mix. The divorce rate on the force might be high, but it was nowhere near a hundred percent.

After he'd been waiting out front for half an hour or so, Celeste emerged from the building.

He simply watched her at first—aware that she seemed even more beautiful than she had only yesterday—then he started toward her.

"Hi," he said, falling into step beside her.

Celeste hadn't noticed Travis until he spoke, and it amazed her that the mere sound of his voice could brighten her mood.

"Hi yourself," she said. "What are you doing here?"

"Oh, I just happened to be in the neighborhood so I figured I'd give you a ride home."

"Just happened to, huh?"

She shot him a smile, then waited, expecting him to ask about her appointment with Walter Namouth. He fooled her, though, and didn't say another word until they'd reached his car.

After sticking the key in the ignition, he looked over at her and said, "You wanted me to let you know about your brother's autopsy. It's today."

"Oh," she murmured, her throat suddenly tight.

"So you can firm up the funeral arrangements for any day from tomorrow on," he added gently.

"Yes. I guess…he wanted to be cremated. Did I mention that?"

"No."

"Well, he did. He told me after our mother died. So instead of a funeral I should really be calling it a memorial service. But as for the time…Saturday, do you think?"

He nodded, hesitated, finally said, "I'd like to go to it with you, but I can't. There'll be guys from Homicide there. Checking out the mourners. It's standard procedure. And as long as you're a suspect, I'd be in hot water if I…"

"I understand," she said. She wished he could be with her, though—so much that it frightened her, because it wasn't a wish that was consistent with the decision she'd come to last night.

After hours of thinking, she'd concluded the only thing to do was keep their relationship platonic. At least until she no longer *was* a suspect.

Once her life was back to some semblance of normality, she'd be in a better position to figure out whether her feelings for him were the genuine item or she merely wanted a strong man to lean on.

Yet, despite knowing it wouldn't be a good idea to—

"But you'll have someone there with you?" he asked.

"Yes. I have an aunt. My mother's sister.

I'm close to her—and to my cousins. And I know some of my friends will come."

"Good." He gave her a reassuring smile. "Would you like to grab an early lunch?"

"Thanks, but I'd better go straight home. I should call and firm up the arrangements for the service. Get it over with. And someone's stopping by for that manuscript."

"Right." He pulled into the flow of traffic. "What about dinner? Are we still on for that or...?"

"Sure," she said, even though she knew finalizing those arrangements wouldn't leave her in the best of spirits. "I'll be better off going out than sitting home alone."

He drove another block or so before finally asking how her meeting with Namouth had gone.

"Well...I'm glad I talked to him, although I couldn't really tell him much. Just that the police thought there'd been a woman at Steve's apartment on Saturday evening, and I've gathered she's a suspect. And that Hank must figure she was me because...

"I explained about the survivor clause in my mother's will. Even though you didn't say exactly *why* Hank figures I did it, there's nothing else I can think of."

Travis still didn't tell her whether she was guessing right or not. He merely said, "And what did Namouth say?"

"He asked how I knew Hank suspected me."

"And?"

"I said you'd warned me. I knew it was safe enough. That lawyer-client privilege would apply to everything I told him.

"His view," she continued unhappily, "is that since there's no one to back up my alibi I'll almost certainly end up having to go in for questioning. Unless the police learn who that woman actually was."

Travis gave her a sympathetic glance, then said, "Well, as I told you yesterday, being questioned and being charged are two very different things. But I assume he advised you not to answer any questions unless he's present?"

"Yes. And he gave me the number of his service. Said they can reach him twenty-four hours a day."

"Well, nobody's going to drag you down to the precinct in the middle of the night. You don't have to worry about that happening."

"No. Of course not."

Still, that hardly meant she didn't have to

worry at all. Being a murder suspect, even an innocent one, was something she couldn't imagine anyone not worrying about.

CHAPTER SEVEN

Wednesday, October 6, 11:28 a.m.

TRAVIS AND CELESTE had just about reached her place when his cellular rang.

"Quinn," he answered.

"I need to talk to you," Hank said with no preamble and an unusual edge to his voice. "Can you meet me at Lucy's? Half an hour?"

"Sure. What's up?"

"I'll fill you in then."

"That was Hank," Travis said, clicking off. "Oh?"

Celeste was obviously going for casual, but her expression said she was dying to ask if the call had been about her brother's case.

"Just wants to meet me for lunch," he told her.

"Oh."

He pulled up in front of her building, parking in the No Standing zone outside the entrance. "I'll see you in."

"You don't have to bother. I'll—"

"It's no bother."

A buzzer system wasn't much of a challenge to anyone with determination, and he hadn't forgotten that Evan Reese knew where Celeste lived. It wouldn't be a surprise to find him lying in wait for her, ostensibly wanting to talk more about their "cosmic connectedness."

There was no sign of Reese, though. Neither on the street nor inside.

"Do you have time to kill before you meet Hank?" Celeste asked, unlocking her door. "Would you like to come in for coffee?"

He'd love to. However, since Hank's tone had warned him that the sooner he heard about whatever was going on the better, he said, "Thanks, but I should just hit the road. I'll see you later."

When she smiled, it almost made him decide he'd stay for a few minutes. Then his feeling about "the sooner the better" made him turn and start down the hall.

On the way to Lucy's, he concluded that Hank was hot to tell him about one of two things: either something major had happened in the department, or there was a new development in the Parker case. He figured the latter was the more likely, but exactly what kind of development?

Not one that proved Celeste's innocence. Not considering how Hank had sounded. So had his partner uncovered more "evidence" pointing in the direction of her guilt?

He really hoped that wasn't it, because if you added enough pieces of circumstantial evidence together you could often build a pretty solid case. And Celeste wasn't guilty. Knowing her as well as he did now, he didn't have even the slightest lingering doubt.

When he arrived at Lucy's, Hank was already there, a mug of coffee in front of him.

"Hey," Travis said, sliding into the booth.

"Hey."

He waited while the waitress brought him coffee, then said, "So? What's been going on?"

"Oh, there's some stuff I want to breeze by you. See what you think."

Travis nodded. Hank had only agreed to keep him informed, but they were so used to bouncing ideas off each other that it would be tough to quit cold turkey.

"First off," he began, "we talked to Rhonda Stirling."

"Jill Flores's friend."

"Right. And their stories match. Had dinner together, watched *The English Patient,* Stirling was there until after midnight. Plus, she took a taxi home and the pickup and drop-off addresses were logged in. So, since Flores wasn't the blonde who was visiting Parker—"

"You mean, the blonde you *assume* was visiting Parker."

Hank shrugged. "She wasn't visiting anyone else. But I want to tell you about a couple of other things before we get to Celeste Langley."

Even though Travis would far rather hear what Hank had to say about Celeste right now, he merely nodded again.

"Most of the neighbors weren't any help. Parker kept pretty much to himself and they barely knew him."

"So you didn't luck out and find one with a motive for killing him."

"No, but his next-door neighbor had an interesting story—and my guess is that Evan Reese is the central figure in it."

"Yeah?"

"Uh-huh. Apparently, one of the good doctor's patients used to show up at his apartment outside of office hours. Must have had a talent for slipping past the concierge. Or maybe he'd discovered another way in. Whichever, he fits Reese's description."

Travis could feel his heart beating a little faster. He'd realized from the start that Reese was bad news, but there'd been nothing to make him think the guy could be their killer. Not until now.

"The neighbor doesn't know how frequently Reese came by," Hank was saying. "Assuming it actually *was* him. But a couple of times Parker wasn't home and Reese ended up pounding on the door, yelling that he needed to talk. That's how this guy could give me a description. The first time he went out into the hall and told Reese to knock it off."

"Only the first time?"

"Yeah, he said our boy got pretty nasty, so the next time he just waited and spoke to Parker about it later."

"But Parker was home on Saturday night," Travis said, thinking aloud. "He'd have let Reese in. And Reese is about five-seven or -eight."

"You figure that didn't occur to me?"

Travis grinned. "I know it did. So have you paid him another visit?"

"Not yet, but I will."

"He'll have a good alibi."

"Probably, but we'll see just how solid it is."

"So…you're looking at the first deputy police commissioner's nephew as a murder suspect. That's almost enough to make me glad Espizito yanked me off the case."

"I'm half wishing he'd yanked me, too. I'll bet Reese makes another call to his uncle after I talk to him again. But at least I'll be able to say he's not the only one we're questioning. We put Parker's name out on the street and came up with another couple of suspects."

"Uh-huh?" They often turned to snitches when they were short of leads. And with surprising frequency, one of their informants would learn something that explained why the victim had been murdered. Maybe he'd lost big at gambling, for example, and hadn't paid up.

"Parker was an amateur musician," Hank was saying. "Used to jam at a club down on Third. And a month or so ago, while the group was taking a break, he ended up sitting by a couple of two-bit crooks who were discussing a string of break-ins they'd pulled off.

"Long story short, Parker called the cops

and they were waiting for the perps when they left the club. 'Course, they made bail the next day, which means they were out when he was killed."

"They knew he'd fingered them?"

Hank nodded. "Apparently, they were drunk enough to be mouthing off, but not too drunk to miss him listening in. They stopped when they noticed, but he'd already heard enough.

"According to our informant, they put things together and were talking revenge. But it might have been nothing more than talk."

"You've got good descriptions, though? Know how tall they are?"

"Not tall."

"So they fit the bill there. But if they'd come to Parker's apartment, he wouldn't have let them in."

"Not likely, although you never know. There could be some explanation. At any rate, we sure want to have a chat with them."

"You know where they are?"

"No. But we'll keep looking till we find them. So what do you think?"

Travis shrugged. "Reese is unstable and I'd say potentially dangerous. But without anyone to put him at the scene, if he's got an alibi that checks out…"

"And the lowlifes?"

"Well, you don't have enough to draw any conclusions there yet. But you already knew that. And you knew my read on Reese, too. So what else are we doing here?"

Hank took a sip of coffee, then met Travis's gaze. "Where do things stand between you and Celeste Langley?"

"I've been seeing her," he admitted. He trusted Hank not to repeat that. And there was undoubtedly a good reason for his question.

"Yeah, I figured you would be. That's why I wanted to tell you about Reese and the scumbags before we got to her.

"I'm going to need some help from you, buddy, and I wanted you concentrating on what I was saying—so you'd have a clear picture of where the *entire* case stands. Because the others are obviously more probable suspects than she is."

"Obviously," Travis said, glad to hear that Hank no longer sounded as if he actually thought Celeste might be a killer.

"I still want to know who that blonde was," he said, shooting Travis a glance that said he hadn't *completely* eliminated Celeste as a possibility.

"But...look," he continued, "I learned something only an hour ago that's started me thinking maybe nobody on my list had anything to do with Parker's death. Neither Celeste nor Reese nor the other two.

"And it's got me back to wondering if Adele Langley's hit-and-run really was an accident. Back to wondering if it's connected to her son's murder. But whether it is or not..."

"Hank, get to the point, huh?"

"Okay, the point is that I put Celeste's name out on the street, too."

"And?" Travis could feel that all-too-familiar numbness at the base of his spine. What had Hank learned about Celeste?

"She was our only suspect at that stage, and I figured it was worth a shot. You never know what you'll hear, right?"

"What did you hear?"

"Buddy...she's in one truckload of trouble."

AFTER CELESTE had spoken with someone at the funeral home and arranged a time for the service on Saturday, she called the relatives and a couple of friends she'd promised to get back to. She'd barely finished that when her intercom buzzed.

It proved to be Travis—even though she hadn't been expecting to see him again until seven.

She released the front-door lock, wondering if he'd figured she'd be feeling blue and in need of company. But whatever he was doing here, just knowing that he was on his way up to her apartment made her smile.

That, however, was *not* good. Ensuring their relationship remained platonic would be tough if he kept showing up every time she turned around. Because the more she saw of him the more she liked him.

She opened her door to discover he was already on his way down the hall. And something obviously wasn't right.

There was tension in his stride, and his expression was so dark that fear began nibbling at her.

For a moment, she felt certain Hank had said he was going to arrest her. But that couldn't be it when she hadn't even been questioned. Could it?

She let Travis in without a word, afraid to ask what the problem was. Instead, she simply led the way to the living room, aware she was only delaying the inevitable.

When he silently sank onto the couch and gestured for her to join him, she made herself ask what was wrong.

He shook his head, looking as if he knew he had to tell her but seriously didn't want to.

"Travis, I can see it's bad, so let's get it over with."

The glance he gave her warned it was even worse than she could imagine.

After a few endless seconds, he said, "I've been trying to think of a good way to say this, but there just isn't one. Hank wanted to see me because he'd learned that…Celeste, somebody's got a contract out on you."

His words hung between them, their meaning not sinking in right away.

When it finally did, her heart began to pound and the room started to spin.

A second later, Travis had his arm around her shoulders and was telling her to put her head between her knees.

"Good. Now, take a few deep breaths," he ordered.

She tried to. But the terror crawling around inside her chest kept clutching at her throat—

and she had to concentrate to breathe at all, let alone deeply.

"It's going to be okay," he said. "I won't let anything happen to you."

She managed another breath, wishing she could believe him yet knowing she'd be incredibly naive to.

"Once you calm down we'll talk. Figure out who's behind this and how to take care of it."

Could they actually do that? Was there even the slightest chance she wouldn't end up dead?

She had no idea how they could possibly "take care of it," but Travis sounded as if he really thought there'd be a way. So maybe, just maybe...

Her heart still thudding and her breathing nowhere near back to normal, she shakily sat up straight.

He gave her an encouraging smile. But instead of making her feel better, it started tears stinging her eyes.

"Oh, Celeste," he murmured as they spilled over. Then he pulled her into his arms and simply held her.

Even someone who wasn't normally a crier had a limit, and she knew she was beyond hers. She cried so hard and for so long that she wasn't sure she'd ever be able to stop.

All the horrible things that had happened during the past year had depleted her emotional reserves, and she was afraid she didn't have enough left to cope with a broken fingernail, let alone the fact that someone wanted her dead.

Gradually, though, she managed to regain control and just sat in the comforting warmth of Travis's embrace.

"All right now?" he murmured at last.

"Yes," she said.

Travis exhaled slowly, feeling strangely bereft as Celeste eased away from him. Her softness made him wish he could hold her forever; her sultry scent was positively bewitching. And now, gazing at her face, he had an almost overwhelming urge to kiss her.

He told himself that was crazy. Her eyes were puffy and her cheeks tear-stained.

Even so, there was something about her that made him want to just take her in his arms again and hold her until she forgot about everything in the world except him.

But she was both terrified and vulnerable, as he'd known she'd be. And during the drive here he'd vowed he would act strictly as a friend to her while she was in that condition.

Besides which, a few other factors were giving him pause. In his more lucid moments, he kept remembering cops and serious relationships didn't mix. And remembering that was why he'd always made a point of backing off whenever he'd felt much more than a twinge of interest in a woman.

So even though Celeste had gotten to him in a way no other woman ever had, if he was smart he'd at least proceed very slowly and carefully.

He'd be crazy to let himself get in any deeper before he had a clearer picture of what she was really like, and what they might be like together.

And getting romantically involved with her would definitely be getting in deeper. So deep, he suspected, that getting out again would prove very difficult. If not impossible.

"Travis?" she said at last. "Are you *sure* about this contract? Couldn't Hank be wrong?"

As much as he wished that was likely, there wasn't much chance of it. And he didn't intend to lie to her. Downplaying how serious things were would be deadly dangerous.

"Hank's not wrong very often," he made

himself say. "And in this instance, he got the word from one of his most reliable sources."

"Then—"

"But contracts can be called off."

"Really?"

Her hopeful look went straight to his heart.

"Really," he said. "A hit man gets paid up front. So if whoever paid him changes his mind, what does he care? He's already got his money."

"Then…there's actually a chance you could…"

"A very *good* chance," he told her, sounding a lot more confident than he felt.

The truth was, he couldn't do a thing about the contract unless he knew either who'd paid for it or who the hit man was. And Hank's informant didn't have a clue about the guy's real identity. He'd only heard him referred to as the Ice Man.

Still, there was nothing to gain by dwelling on the negative. Especially not when, with any luck, he and Celeste would be able to figure out who'd hired the killer. Or at least come up with a probable suspect.

Telling himself it was time to get started on that, he said, "Celeste, I know this is an awful question, but I have to ask it. Can you think of anyone who might want you dead?"

While she stared at her shoes, he rapidly reminded himself how far he'd decided to go here.

He wasn't about to get into the possibility that her mother's "accident" had been step one in somebody's plan to murder *three* people. Not yet, at least. It would only make her more upset.

Besides, after Hank talked to the investigating officers and learned what the witnesses had to say, he might conclude that Adele Langley's death really *had* been accidental.

Regardless of that, though, the important thing right now was to figure out who was targeting Celeste.

Finally, she looked up again, her blue eyes dark with emotion, and said, "Travis, I honestly don't have a clue who'd want to kill me."

"No, I didn't really think you would," he said softly. "But somebody *does,* and he's got to have a reason. And…Hank has a theory about that."

"What is it?"

"Well…this entire conversation has to stay

strictly between the two of us. You understand that."

"Of course. I know you could get in trouble, and I'd never say anything to... You can trust me."

He nodded, certain he could, yet feeling strange about the prospect of letting a civilian in on confidential police business.

That wasn't how he'd originally intended to play things with her. And under normal circumstances he'd never have changed his mind. But these were hardly normal circumstances, so he simply ignored the uneasy feeling and began.

"Hank figures that whoever killed Steve is behind the contract on you."

"What?" she whispered, her face growing pale.

After hesitating a second, he took her hands in his. Trying to comfort her hardly constituted as a romantic gesture.

She gazed at him for a long moment, then slowly shook her head. "I don't understand. Are you saying Steve was murdered by this hit man who—"

"No, he was killed by an amateur."

"How do you know?"

"I'm a detective," he said, hoping she'd let it

go at that. When she was already in a fragile state, hearing additional details about Parker's death wouldn't help.

"But how can you be *sure?*"

He hesitated again, then decided that telling her she didn't need to know would be so patronizing it might only upset her more.

"Because a pro is concerned about the risk of getting caught," he said. "So he chooses his time and place carefully. He doesn't want witnesses. He just wants to do the job and get away from the scene as quickly as possible. That's why he'll often shoot someone in a drive-by or do it in a deserted underground garage."

"What about those killings you see on the news? Where somebody gets murdered right out in the open? In broad daylight?"

"Those are usually mob or gang related. And they *want* witnesses because they're sending a message.

"But we're talking about someone who makes his living as a professional killer. Someone who'd rather not try sneaking into a secure apartment building like your brother's, hoping he can get up to the fifth floor and back down again without anyone seeing him.

"Plus, he uses a serious weapon. He doesn't take any chances on his victim living to tell tales. Whereas Steve was killed with a small pistol. A .38 caliber."

"It was big enough to do the job," she murmured.

"I...Celeste, I'm sorry. I didn't mean to sound as if I'm minimizing what happened to him. I was only explaining how we know an amateur killed him."

She slowly shook her head. "But an amateur kills him, then turns around and hires a hit man to kill me? Does that make sense? I mean, I live alone. And a woman would generally be an easier target than a man, wouldn't she? So why...?"

"I don't know," he admitted. "The best Hank and I could come up with is that whoever's behind this just decided not to press his luck."

"But...couldn't it be that the contract *isn't* connected to Steve's death?"

"It's not *entirely* out of the question. Hank and his team are following up on a couple of other possibilities."

"You mean other suspects."

"Yes."

"Who?"

"That doesn't really matter, so—"

"But it *does!* Oh, I know you're the expert here, but I'm the one somebody wants dead. And I need you to tell me every detail you can.

"It… Huh, I was about to say it would make me feel better, and that would be ridiculous. Right now, I don't know what would make me feel better. But maybe something will strike a chord, because I'm part of whatever's going on."

He realized she could be right. She was coming at this from an entirely different perspective, so she might think of something he wouldn't.

"Okay," he said, then proceeded to give her a bare-bones summary of the stories about the burglars Parker overheard in the club and Evan Reese showing up at his door.

"Hasn't Hank taken Reese in for questioning?" she asked when he was done.

"Not yet. There's an added wrinkle with him. His uncle happens to be the first deputy police commissioner."

"Ah. So *that's* how he managed to cause you so much trouble."

"Exactly. And now that we know who his uncle Fred is, Hank will handle him more carefully than I did. But Reese and the others may turn out to have airtight alibis. And if they do...

"Well, let's get back to the likelihood that the contract's connected to your brother's murder. When his death means you inherit everything from your mother's estate, the obvious question is who would benefit if you died?"

"I..."

"Do you have a will?"

"Yes, but—"

"Who's your beneficiary?" He waited as she anxiously licked her lips—praying she'd give him a name, that she hadn't bequeathed everything to some charitable organization.

"My husband," she murmured at last.

CHAPTER EIGHT

Wednesday, October 6, 4:21 p.m.

HER HUSBAND. Her estranged husband who was living with another woman. Travis's thoughts had begun racing so fast they all deserved speeding tickets.

"But…Bryce would never in a million years have murdered Steve," Celeste murmured. "Or hired a hit man to kill me."

He nodded slowly, as if buying that, but he was actually recalling she'd mentioned that Bryce had offered his help when her mother died. And phoned her just the other day, after he'd "heard" about Steve.

Of course, the guy could have been calling out of genuine concern. Or maybe he'd had another reason.

He might have just been keeping in touch, making sure she didn't suddenly decide to get away from her problems and take off. That she'd be where they were expecting her to be when the hit man came calling.

Focusing on her again, he said, "Celeste, is Bryce aware he's your beneficiary?"

She gnawed on her lower lip for a moment, then said, "Yes. In fact, he drew up the wills. Shortly after we got married. His specialty is estate law."

"You said wills? Plural?" Travis asked, telling himself to proceed as coolly as he would in any other interview situation.

"Yes. Two. Mine and my mother's."

"So...the survivor clause was his idea?"

"I'm not sure. Probably, though. Knowing my mother, she'd have left the details up to him."

"Look...I'm going to ask you something you might think is none of my business. But how much is that estate worth? More or less."

"I'm not exactly sure yet. It's a few hundred thousand dollars, though."

He didn't press for anything more specific. "A few" left a lot of leeway, yet even as few as three was significant money.

"Would Bryce know the amount?"

Celeste shook her head. "My parents weren't the sort of people who talked about their finances."

"Still, after the will was filed he could have learned roughly how much was involved. And sometimes," he added quietly, "greed makes a man do things no one would have ever imagined him doing."

"Travis…Bryce just *couldn't* be the one. But there's something I might as well tell you right now. He doesn't have any more of an alibi than I do for Saturday night."

His adrenaline began pumping harder. "How do you know?"

"Because when he phoned to offer his condolences, he happened to mention he'd been home alone. Donna Rainfield has a part in a play, so she wasn't there. But…that really just reinforces the fact he *didn't* do it. If he *had* he'd have a solid alibi. Bryce is an intelligent man. He'd cover himself."

Travis nodded once more, thinking that even intelligent men sometimes do foolish things. Or maybe Bryce figured that going with the home-alone story was smarter than concocting an alibi that would mean relying on someone else to lie.

A liar could always change his tune. Or try his hand at blackmail a few miles down the road.

"Let's play around with the possibility it

was Bryce," he said. "Even if you're sure it couldn't have been," he interrupted when Celeste started to say something. "Just let me ask you a couple of questions. How tall is he?"

She hesitated, as if uncertain she was willing to "play around" with this at all, but finally said, "Not very. In heels, I'm as tall as him. Why?"

"We don't think whoever killed your brother was very tall."

"Oh. But—"

"And what if he'd called Steve, said he wanted to talk to him about something. Would Steve have told him to come over?"

"Yes, of course," she said slowly. "You know...this should have occurred to me before, but didn't the concierge remember sending anyone up to Steve's apartment that night?"

Travis shook his head. "Which probably means the killer either snuck past him or got in a back way. Otherwise, it would have had to be someone already in the building."

"Like a neighbor, you mean."

"Yes, but all the neighbors have been interviewed and none of them seems to have an even remote motive."

Whereas the case against Bryce was looking awfully strong. When he drew up those wills, his marriage to Celeste had been intact. And if he actually was capable of murder, in the back of his mind he'd have been thinking that when Adele Langley died he'd ensure something happened to her son shortly thereafter.

Now, though, the marriage was over. So for Bryce to get his hands on any of the money something would have to happen to Celeste, as well.

"But...isn't that kind of a standard thing?" she said. "The survivor clause," she added at his puzzled glance.

"I'm not sure."

"Well, whether it is or not, Bryce just isn't a man who'd ever... Besides, he has to assume I've had a new will written. Naming a new beneficiary. I mean, I should have. Months ago. I just haven't gotten around to it."

After considering that, Travis said, "I need to make a call."

SNOOPS HAD WANDERED into the living room, his desire for attention apparently stronger than his wariness of Travis, so Celeste sat stroking him while she waited for Travis to finish his conversation.

He'd phoned a lawyer he played handball with and explained the situation. Now he wasn't talking, was just listening to what his friend had to say.

As the silence lengthened, she couldn't stop herself from contemplating the possibility that Bryce really might have killed Steve.

Initially, she'd found the idea beyond belief, had been certain she couldn't have been married to someone for three years without suspecting he was that morally corrupt.

Oh, she knew from personal experience he was hardly the most principled man in the world. But cheating on her wasn't in the same league as murdering her brother and hiring someone to kill her. Just the thought of that…

She swallowed hard, feeling physically ill.

"I'm not sure," Travis said into the phone. Then he glanced at her. "Have either of you started divorce proceedings?"

"No. I mean, I guess Bryce *might* have, but I'm pretty sure he'd have let me know before he did."

Of course, maybe she shouldn't be too sure

about *anything* when it came to Bryce. And now that she was thinking about it, it seemed a little surprising that he hadn't pressed the issue. Because she'd gathered that Donna Rainfield would like nothing better than to become wife number two.

Not that she knew Donna personally. They'd never actually met. But a few weeks after she'd left Bryce, one of his "friends" had invited her to dinner—then hit on her during dessert.

Before that, though, over the main course, he'd insisted on telling her all about Donna. And she sounded like the sort of woman who'd be thrilled to have a lawyer for a husband. Apparently, she had much more expensive tastes than an off-Broadway actress could indulge.

As for herself, she'd gotten as far as making an appointment with a divorce lawyer. But before she'd seen him her mother had been killed, and she just hadn't done any more about it yet.

"Celeste?" Travis said, interrupting her reverie. "You don't have children, do you?"

"No," she said again, wondering if he imagined she had a couple hidden in a closet.

Then, as he was telling his friend she had none, she realized that, conceivably, she might have some who were living with Bryce.

Absently, she brushed her hair away from her face, thinking how very little she and Travis actually knew about each other. From there, her thoughts went scurrying back to what she'd been wondering about, on and off, from the first moment she'd realized how drawn she was to him.

Was she falling for the man himself, or for the emotional anchor he represented?

She was no closer to answering that question than she'd been in the beginning. Of course, if she ended up dead, the answer would be irrelevant.

As the truth of that sent a shiver all the way to her toes, Travis thanked his friend and clicked off.

"Okay, here's the deal," he said, setting the cordless on the coffee table. "As long as you're still legally married to Bryce and you're childless, he's entitled to half your estate if you die. That would be true even if you'd signed a new will that left him nothing."

"But that isn't right. I mean, it *shouldn't* be."

"Well, according to New York State law it

is. All he'd have to do is file some forms in probate court. A procedure called 'electing against the will.'"

She hadn't known that, but Bryce would have.

"What did he tell you about the survivor clause?" she asked. "*Is* it a standard sort of thing?"

"Not when a mother's leaving her estate to her offspring. It's only standard in wills drawn up for a husband and wife—in case they're in an accident together and both die."

"But…if it's common in at least some wills, Bryce probably just put it in because he was covering all the bases. He's picky about details."

Travis was silent for a minute. "Celeste," he said at last, "*someone* wants you dead badly enough that he's paid a hit man to make it happen. And thus far, the only person we know would gain from your death is Bryce."

"Yes, but…" She paused, considering just how *much* he'd gain.

Her automatic reaction, when Travis had asked her what the estate was worth, had been to hedge a bit.

As she'd told him, her parents hadn't been

the sort of people who'd talked about their finances. And neither was she.

Besides, she honestly *didn't* know the exact number yet. And even though she could have been a little more specific, she doubted it mattered.

The key thing was that he'd assumed it was enough to interest Bryce—and it would be.

Bryce made a lot of money, but he spent a lot, too. He liked the best of everything. And he must have told her a hundred times that he should have gone to medical school rather than law school because he'd be earning far more if he had.

"Look," Travis said, "I'll fill Hank in and he'll start doing the *official* digging around about Bryce. But if there's anything more I can come up with that might help, I will."

"It doesn't sound as if you're really considering yourself off the case."

"No. By the time Hank and I finished talking, we decided that he'll keep sharing information with me and I'll share whatever I can learn with him. But he's got to focus on nailing whoever killed your brother, while I'm going to concentrate on the contract. I'll track down his informant, see if I can get a lead on who this Ice Man is."

She nodded, then said, "What about me as a suspect? Does Hank still think there's a chance I did it?"

"No. Since he heard about the contract, he's dropped the odds on that to one in a million. And as soon as I tell him about Bryce, he'll be the primary suspect.

"Of course, if it turns out he's *not* behind it... But it seems so obvious. And if we can turn up something that points more directly to him..."

"And if you can't?"

"Hank will talk to him, anyway."

"And say?"

"It depends. Maybe just come right out and tell him that somebody's put a contract on you. See how he reacts."

"Really?"

"Uh-huh. We do virtually anything we think might help us. And that includes telling a suspect facts about a case. Because if he's guilty, he already knows them. And if he's not, it usually doesn't matter."

"Ah."

"But, look, while we're trying to get to the bottom of things, you can't stay here. This Ice Man will know where you live, and we sure don't want him watching you coming and going."

Her mouth went dry. She knew what Travis actually meant. They didn't want him lurking in the street outside so he could shoot her when she walked out the front door. Or want him following her, just waiting for an opportune moment.

"No...no, of course I can't stay here," she murmured. "But where should I go?"

"You should come stay with me."

IT WAS ONLY THREE or four miles from the Upper West Side down to Chelsea, where Travis lived, yet in the rush-hour traffic Celeste guessed they'd be a good hour getting there. And the cat was doing his utmost to make her feel as if the trip might take forever.

Snoops was yeowling at full volume, protesting the torture of being confined in his carrier and forced to ride in a car. The hubbub outside—Manhattan going about its routine business—was a murmur in comparison.

"Does he do that very often?" Travis asked, glancing across at her.

He merely seemed curious, not perturbed about the possibility, but he had to be worried that he'd let himself in for some sleepless nights.

"Almost never," she assured him. "Only in cars. He won't be a problem in your apartment. Really."

He nodded, then checked the rearview mirror again.

She resisted the urge to turn around and have her own look. There was simply no way the Ice Man could be following them.

Before she'd come out of her building, Travis had walked both sides of her entire block—peering into each parked car and every space where someone might have been concealed.

So the hit man couldn't have been watching and seen them leave. But if Travis was positive of that, what was he so concerned about?

When he checked the mirror yet again, she said, "Do you think he could be back there?"

"No."

"Then why do you keep looking?"

"Just habit."

As they were inching ahead another couple of feet, the driver next to them leaned on his horn. The sudden blare made her jump, even though she was normally oblivious to the constant noises of the city.

"Celeste," Travis said quietly, "you're going to be okay. He won't have the slightest idea where to find you."

"He'll try to, though," she murmured, wishing she felt a lot braver than she did.

"Yeah, he'll try. But none of your friends or relatives even know I exist. So as long as you don't tell anyone where you are, you'll be perfectly safe."

Perfectly safe. She surreptitiously glanced at his chiseled profile, thinking that whether he was right depended—at least in part—on how she defined the term.

She was very aware that staying with him would *not* be conducive to keeping things platonic between them. Yet what else could she do?

She certainly couldn't have asked one of her friends to put her up. Not when she'd have had to say, "Oh, and by the way, if anyone knocks on the door while I'm here, don't answer. Because it might be a hit man."

And she'd ruled out the idea of going to a hotel. She'd be scared to death on her own. Whereas with Travis…well, she expected she'd only be scared half to death at his place.

She sat staring out the car window, aware she'd never felt like such a 'fraidy-cat before.

Not in her entire life. She was a New Yorker, and growing up in this city taught you to be self-assured and resourceful.

So what was the matter with her?

That was hardly a tough question to answer. She was probably still in a state of shock. After all, learning there was a contract on your life was hardly an everyday occurrence.

But she didn't have to deal with the situation alone. She had Travis—thankfully.

And the hit man *wouldn't* be able to find her. She'd already called her aunt and a couple of friends to say she was going to visit a girlfriend in Connecticut. That she would come back into the city for Steve's service, then be gone again. So her cover story was in place. Now all she had to do was be patient while Travis got to the bottom of things.

Which meant that feeling so frightened was positively stupid. Instead of giving in to her anxiety, she should be making every effort to carry on as usual.

Well, not *exactly* as usual. She knew she wouldn't be able to stop worrying entirely. And she'd be laying low. But if that was all it took to keep safe…

She almost smiled. She was thinking

straight again, and it felt a whole lot better than having her head filled with fears.

"About Hank?" she said, telling herself that carrying on as usual included having normal conversations.

"What about him?" Travis asked.

"Are you going to tell him I'm staying with you?"

"Uh-huh. And he'll get a big kick out of it."

"Oh? Why?"

He shrugged, his expression sheepish. "He knows I like you."

"You do?" she teased—then congratulated herself on managing to.

"Very funny," he muttered. "You think I'd invite just any woman to stay with me? Especially one with a cat?" he added as Snoops let out a particularly sharp wail.

She actually did smile then. He'd been making the fact that he liked her perfectly obvious, of course, but his coming right out and saying so had her suddenly feeling a lot better about this mess she was in. There might not be a logical reason it should, but it did.

After a minute or two of silence, she said, "Travis...I really, really appreciate what you're doing for me. Without you..."

She warned herself to stop right there. She

was tempted to tell him she liked him, too. Liked him very much. But until she was sure *why* she did, she had to be careful. Otherwise, when this was all over she might realize... No, the last thing she wanted to end up doing was hurting him.

Reaching over, he rested his hand on hers. "You know, things aren't anywhere near as bad as they seem. As I told you before, either we learn who this Ice Man is and take him off the street, or we establish who's behind the contract. Then, before we arrest him, he calls it off."

"You make it sound so simple."

"Yeah, well, if I'm right, if Bryce is responsible, it will be."

"But even if it *is* him, he won't admit it. And he's smart enough that there'll be nothing to link him to—"

"Celeste, I make my living finding out things people don't want me to know. So trust me."

"I do," she murmured.

"Good."

He gave her hand a squeeze, then put his own back on the steering wheel.

She wished he hadn't. His touch was reassuring, and she was nowhere near the point of not needing reassurance.

Thinking that she'd just have to keep on psyching herself up, she gazed out into the gathering dusk.

Down the block, a young mother was pushing a baby in a stroller and trying to prevent her dog from wrapping its leash around her legs.

Watching her made Celeste wonder if she'd live long enough to have the children she'd always wanted. Or even long enough to fall in love with a potential father.

Then she looked back at Travis and was suddenly imagining *herself* pushing a stroller—occupied by a little boy with big dark eyes.

WHEN TRAVIS HAD told her he lived in Chelsea, a few blocks south of Madison Square Garden, Celeste had pictured a somewhat tired old apartment building. In reality, his place was half the second floor of a nineteenth-century town house that had been renovated into a fourplex.

He unlocked the door and switched on a light, then ushered her inside, setting her suitcase and the shopping bag full of Snoops's things on the floor.

She put down the cat carrier—suddenly feeling even more nervous about the prospect of staying here with him.

"I'm afraid it's not very big," he said.

"Hey, this is Manhattan. I have friends living with people they absolutely abhor, because they can't find anything they can afford on their own."

Travis shot her a smile. "Yeah, you're right. Actually, I know I was lucky to get it. The leasing manager is a friend of a friend, so I had the inside track. At any rate, if you take the bedroom we should be—"

"Oh, no, I can't put you out like that. I—"

"Celeste, it'll be the best arrangement. Cops have trouble sleeping. It's a shift-work thing. And when I can't sleep I watch TV. There isn't one in the bedroom."

"But—"

"I'll be fine. I've drifted off on that couch a thousand times. It's really pretty comfortable."

It was an oversize, overstuffed piece covered in fabric the color of denim. And it *did* look comfortable. Even so, she felt guilty.

"Well…if you're sure."

"Of course I'm sure."

Forcing a smile, she gazed around. The room was sparsely furnished and decidedly masculine, its pale gray walls decorated with framed charcoal sketches.

A gray coffee table sat in front of the couch and a black leather recliner faced the television set. On the end table next to the chair sat a cordless phone, an Elmore Leonard novel and a couple of hand weights.

There was no challenge to picturing Travis in the recliner watching the Yankees. Or a football game. Or…

As she realized she had no idea what his favorite sport was, or even if he *was* a sports fan, the thought that they didn't really know much about each other drifted through her mind once more.

The truth was that they barely knew anything at all. Yet here she was, come to stay, even though moving into a veritable stranger's place was completely out of character for her.

Seized by a sudden need to put distance between them, she wandered across the room and looked out into the gathering dusk. As she'd noticed when they'd arrived, there was a block of green space on the far side of the street.

"Chelsea Park," Travis said, joining her at the window. "It doesn't exactly rival Central Park, but it's nicer than looking out on a row of buildings."

She nodded slowly, certain he was standing far enough away that she couldn't *actually* have felt the warmth of his breath on her skin. No more than she was really smelling his country-autumn scent or feeling his body heat. But her imagination had shifted into high gear, and she was so conscious of his nearness that her pulse was racing.

Somehow, being alone with him here wasn't the same as being alone with him in *her* apartment. Here, in his own space, he seemed even more take-charge and self-assured—and even more appealing.

She was just telling herself she'd simply have to ignore the pull she felt toward him, when Snoops meowed plaintively from his carrier.

"He's tired of being in there," Travis said.

"Well, when I let him out his priority will be finding a place to hide. So I'd better set up his litter box first. Then I can show him where it is before he disappears. Should I put it in the bathroom?"

"I guess," he said, looking as if he didn't have a clue about cats. "It's the first door down the hall. I'll take this into the bedroom," he added, picking up her suitcase.

By the time she'd finished with the litter box, Travis was back in the living room. He'd removed his jacket—revealing a gun in a shoulder holster.

Fleetingly, she wondered why she hadn't realized he was wearing it when she'd been crying in his arms.

Just the angle it had been at, she decided as he took it off.

"I usually leave this on the bedside table," he told her. "But with you staying in there…"

He paused, eyeing the way she was staring at it. "If I put it here by the phone, it won't bother you, will it?"

"No, it won't bother me." Under different circumstances, it might. But considering she knew someone was out to kill her, she'd be glad it was there.

"Do you know how to use a gun?"

She shook her head.

"Well, I'll show you the basics later. I've got a couple of others, and you might as well keep one close at hand when I'm not here. Just in case."

"Good idea," she murmured, refusing to let herself imagine a "just in case" scenario.

"Oh, and by the way, don't use this phone. Too many people have caller ID."

"I'll only use it to check my answering machine."

"Do *you* have caller ID?"

When she nodded, he said, "Then don't even use it for that. Someone might decide to have a look around your apartment."

"Ah." That thought made her almost as uneasy as the fact that he figured she should have a gun.

"You can use my cell," he added.

Just as he set his gun down by the cordless, it rang.

"Hey, you're getting psychic," Travis said after he picked up. "I was going to call you in a few minutes.

"Yeah?…Sure, I'll be right there.

"That was Hank," he told her, clicking off. "He's only a few blocks away and he's going to stop by."

CHAPTER NINE

Wednesday, October 6, 7:43 p.m.

CELESTE WAITED UNTIL Travis had gone downstairs to let Hank in, then took Snoops into the bathroom and freed him from the carrier. He didn't even glance at the litter box before racing off, but he'd know it was there when he needed it.

It was a good ten minutes before Travis arrived back with Hank, and he apologized for being so long. "I was telling him about Bryce," he explained.

She nodded, recalling he'd said that once he did Bryce would be Hank's prime suspect— as well as Travis's. Somehow, that made the possibility she actually *had* married a man capable of murder, or capable of hiring someone to murder *her,* seem more real.

As she told herself not to dwell on that, Hank said, "Staying here's a good idea. You'll be a lot safer."

Obviously, Travis had also told him about the temporary living arrangements.

"Well, I know I'm imposing, but—"

"You're *not* imposing," Travis interrupted. "I wouldn't have offered unless I'd wanted to."

Something in his tone made her glance up at him, and the warmth in his eyes made mockery of the idea that they could ever be just friends. No matter how hard she worked at it.

Then she glanced at Hank and realized it was even apparent to him.

Their gazes caught for a second before he looked away and said to Travis, "There were a couple of other things I wanted to talk to you about."

"I'll go and unpack," she said.

"No, wait. You might as well stay and hear this. I paid Evan Reese another visit, and found out how he knew about you."

"How?" Travis demanded.

"He poked around in her brother's apartment. Did you tell Celeste about his showing up there?"

"Yeah."

"Well, one time he was there, Parker took a personal call in the bedroom. So Reese poked through what was in the end tables—checked out some snapshots, Parker's address book, things like that."

"What a sleazoid," Travis muttered.

"Yeah, but according to his way of thinking he had every right. He said that since he confided all his secrets to Parker, it was only fair that he got to find out a little about Parker's personal life."

"Kind of a warped view of a relationship with your psychiatrist," Travis said.

"Well, we already knew he was warped. At any rate," Hank continued, focusing on Celeste, "I told him not to contact you again."

"I already did that, remember?" Travis said. "And it didn't help."

Hank grinned. "Yeah, but I told him politely. I didn't threaten to…"

As Hank stopped speaking midsentence, Celeste looked at Travis. "What did you threaten to do?"

He shrugged. "Enough to get myself turfed off the case. But what about an alibi?" he asked Hank. "Does Reese have one?"

"Afraid so. He's definitely not our killer. He was nowhere near Parker's place last Saturday."

"You're sure?"

"Positive. He was on Long Island with his mother. Having dinner at Uncle Fred's."

HANK STAYED for dinner—ordered-in pizzas—then Travis walked him down to the front door.

When he got back to the apartment he discovered that Celeste had the dishes soaking in the sink, had put the empty beer bottles in the carton and was sticking the remains of the pizzas into the fridge.

Her back was to him, and he decided she had to have the loveliest hair in the entire state of New York. Maybe even on the entire East Coast.

As she turned toward him, he said, "You didn't have to do the cleaning up."

"No?" She smiled. "So it's all right if I just move in with my cat and do absolutely nothing to help out?"

He laughed and she smiled again—such a captivating smile that his heart skipped a couple of beats. She walked past him into the living room, giving him a faint whiff of her sultry perfume.

He mentally shook his head, thinking he was growing used to the way he felt about having her around but hadn't really come to terms with it.

His entire adult life, he'd always assumed he could continue on indefinitely, never getting serious about a woman. But that assumption had come crashing down around him when he'd met *this* woman and done an abrupt one-eighty.

He wanted to be with her every minute and thought about her constantly. Last night she'd even been in his dreams.

If those weren't indicators of "serious" he didn't know what would be.

And yet he had to listen to the voice of reason—busily reminding him that going "slowly" and "carefully" with Celeste made sense.

After listening to it for another couple of seconds, he decided it was right. So he'd just have to exercise a little patience and self-control.

With that plan clearly in mind, he headed into the living room and ordered himself to sit in his recliner. Himself, however, completely ignored the order and sank onto the couch beside Celeste.

"How long," she said, "before they catch

up with those two crooks Steve reported to the police?"

"It shouldn't be long. It's not as if our guys don't know who they're looking for."

Of course, Hank had quietly mentioned that neither of the lowlifes had shown up at their apartments last night, which probably meant they'd heard the police wanted to question them. And there were a lot of places they could hide in a city the size of New York.

He wouldn't say that to Celeste, though. She already had more than enough to worry about.

"And if they have alibis?" she asked. "Like Evan Reese? Are there any other suspects, or would that mean the contract is *definitely* connected to Steve's murder?"

He hesitated, trying to figure out exactly what he should tell her.

She appeared to have come to terms with the situation. At least, she no longer seemed nearly as upset about it. But she still had to be pretty frightened. Anyone in her right mind would be.

"Hank hasn't forgotten about the blond woman," he said at last. "And the crime-scene boys might have come up with something of interest. We just won't have the lab results for a while."

"'A while' being?"

"It depends on how backed up they are."

"So...I must be sounding like a broken record, but we won't be *certain* whether the murder and the contract are related until...?"

"Celeste, Hank and I figure it would be a major coincidence if they *aren't*. You already know that. But the important thing is that nothing will come of the contract. I'll make sure you stay perfectly safe."

"You promise?" she murmured.

"Yeah, I promise. I told you before, I'll be doing everything I can to learn who this Ice Man is."

"And what will I be doing?"

For an instant he thought she was trying to be funny, and it must have shown because she said, "Travis, the longer I think about it the more I realize I don't want to just be sitting around your apartment with Snoops. This is *my* problem, and there must be something I can do to help."

He nodded. "I'm sure I'll have more questions you can answer. So will Hank."

"But that's nothing. I feel like some—"

"Celeste, just listen to me, okay? I understand how you feel, but you've got to lie low. Period. There aren't any other options."

"But I—"

"No. Look, I'm a cop. Dealing with things like this is what I do. And I've got contacts on the street. But they're not the sort of people who'd talk to me if you were along. And you certainly can't head off trying to do anything on your own."

"I…" She shook her head. "You're right. Of course you're right. But I hate being so totally dependent on other people. It's frustrating and…and I'm just so scared that…"

"I know," he said softly.

She stared at the floor for several seconds, then gave him the most obviously forced smile he'd ever seen.

"You okay now?" he asked, resisting the urge to take her in his arms.

"More or less. So…where were we before I went off the deep end?"

"I think I just said I'd be trying to learn who this Ice Man is. And whether Bryce really *is* behind things."

"And if it turns out he isn't?"

"I'll keep digging till I learn who is. Or Hank will find out."

He held her gaze for a long moment. Then,

when he tried to let it go, he discovered he couldn't.

"Travis?" she said quietly.

"What?"

"I was so upset earlier that I can't remember. Did I tell you how much I appreciate your helping me? And your letting me stay here?"

"Yeah, you did."

"Good."

He tried again to stop gazing into her eyes—with no more success than he'd had before. There was something positively mesmerizing about their blue depth.

But he could still hear his common sense babbling on about patience and self-control. And telling him that kissing her, right here and now, would *not* be a wise move.

Despite that, he just couldn't stop himself. He reached for her and drew her near.

Her scent enveloped him and she felt so right in his arms. Kissing her was even better than he'd imagined—her lips so warm and soft and smooth that he wanted to kiss her forever.

When she slipped her hands around the back of his neck, pulling his mouth even more closely to hers, his heart slammed against his ribs.

"Travis," she whispered, her breath hot against his mouth.

He kissed her again, more deeply this time, his arms moving to envelop her.

"Travis," she whispered again, drawing back a little and capturing his hands in hers.

He sat motionless, his heart hammering, desperately wanting to pull her back to him but not letting himself.

"Oh, Travis," she murmured. "I knew this was going to happen. I mean, I thought maybe I could keep it from... But I knew I probably couldn't. And...everything's just so complicated already. Without us getting... So as much as I like you..."

Clearing his throat, he told himself he should say something. But he didn't have a clue what.

"I just think," she continued at last, "it would be better if we didn't do this while I'm staying here. That we wait until the...*situation* is resolved and see how we feel then. As I said, things are so complicated already..."

"Right," he managed. "You're right."

"It isn't that I'm not attracted to you. It isn't that at all."

"No. No, of course not. It's only...not sensible to make things any *more* complicated."

"Exactly." She gave him a tiny smile.

"Then...it would be better if we weren't sitting so close."

She nodded, easing off him and scooting a foot or so along the couch.

For a moment, the heat of her body remained part of him. Then it dissipated into the air, leaving him chilled. Once again, he was at a loss for words.

"You know what?" he finally said. "It's been a long day, so I'm going to take a hot shower and turn in early. Unless you want to watch TV," he added as an afterthought.

"No. I'll just curl up in bed with one of the books I brought."

"Oh. Good. Then...I'll go get a few things from the bedroom...have that shower. And I still want to show you how to use a gun before I turn in. I haven't forgotten about that."

Celeste watched Travis head out of the room, wishing with all her heart she'd managed to handle that a whole lot better than she had. She shouldn't have let things progress so far before calling a halt.

But when he'd started kissing her she hadn't wanted him to stop. Goodness, when she'd *told* him to stop she hadn't wanted him to. Not really. Not deep down.

No man had ever made her feel the way he just had—as if she was the most cherished woman in the world.

Cherished. It was such an old-fashioned word, but it perfectly described the way Travis had made her feel. She didn't know quite how he'd done it, but he had.

It was a feeling she wanted to recapture. To hang on to. But given the circumstances...

Exhaling slowly, she assured herself she'd done the right thing, that keeping all this from getting even more complicated was the only rational way to proceed. Yet if it was right, why had it left her feeling so alone and lonely?

Not wanting to even think about the answer to that one, she pushed herself up off the couch and wandered across the living room.

The hum of the city whispered to her through the window. Directly below her, though, West Twenty-eighth was still. On the far side, Chelsea Park lay in silent darkness.

The only movement she could see was the black shadow of a man walking slowly along the edge of the grass. He paused, putting his cigarette to his mouth.

She absently gazed at its tiny red glow. Then, suddenly, he looked in her direction.

It was nothing more than a casual glance, but it was enough to make her shrink from the glass, her heart pounding.

She nervously licked her lips, thinking she *had* been right to stop things with Travis. Regardless of how he made her feel, she was *definitely* in no emotional shape to be even contemplating what she'd been contemplating.

THE ICE MAN took another drag on his cigarette and continued to watch Detective Travis Quinn's window.

Going by the Langley woman's place, again tonight, had been a good idea. And when he'd seen that her apartment was dark, his hunch about driving down here had been even better.

"A homicide detective," he muttered, thinking again that it was a very good thing he'd had Quinn's plate number run.

Once he'd gotten the name and address, filling in the rest of the blanks had been easy. And that had started danger lights flashing in his head.

A run-of-the-mill cop boyfriend would have been bad enough. A homicide detective was that much worse. After she was dead, this guy was gonna pull out all the stops trying to ID her killer.

But at least he knew where things stood. He'd just have to be even more careful than usual.

Not that he was *ever* careless. It was one reason he was the best. Another was that he always learned whatever he needed to know. Left nothing to chance.

Like, with Celeste Langley, he'd have to be able to find her when the time came. And now that he'd been here tonight, he knew if she wasn't at home this would be the next place to check.

Shivering a little in the night air, he turned the collar of his jacket up against the wind and told himself he might as well get going. She wouldn't be reappearing at that window.

She hadn't liked him seeing her. He'd easily read her reaction when she'd spotted him looking. A stranger watching had frightened her.

He smiled, thinking how much *more* frightened she'd be if she knew who he was and why he was here.

"You can run, but you can't hide," he whispered to the night. Then he tossed his cigarette away, jammed his hands into his pockets and started off—trying to put this job out of his mind for the time being, but not entirely able to.

He hated complications. And he *really* hated this one. A homicide detective. Not good.

If he'd known then what he knew now he'd have doubled his price. At least. Actually, he'd probably have turned down the job.

But he hadn't known. And he'd taken the money. So that was that. He'd do what he'd been paid for. Just as soon as he got the go-ahead call.

Turning onto Ninth Avenue, he started hoping it would come soon. The combination of Detective Travis Quinn and having to wait was making him nervous. And he never got nervous. That was why they called him the Ice Man.

TRAVIS CLOSED the front door against the final fingers of twilight and trudged up the stairs.

Arriving home usually lifted his mood if he was down, but not tonight. Because as much as he wished he had good news for Celeste, he didn't. Spending the entire day on the street had basically gotten him nowhere.

He'd located the snitch who'd told Hank

about the contract, but the guy swore he had no idea who the Ice Man was. Or who was paying for the hit. All he'd heard was that a buddy of a buddy—yadda, yadda, yadda.

And the *yadda, yaddas* might be true or they might not. That was how things worked with a rat. You rarely found out where his information came from.

It seldom mattered, though. The important thing was that a snitch made his living by keeping his eyes and ears open. And by being well-enough plugged into the seamier side of the city that he had a few cops who could come to him when they were fishing. The way Hank had with Celeste's name.

Then the snitch found out what he could and you paid him, the amount depending on the value of what he'd learned. And considering how much money Travis had offered for *anything* more about that contract, he was pretty sure the guy really had told all he knew.

The other informants he'd tracked down hadn't done him any good, either. One had admitted to having heard of the Ice Man. But again, only the nickname.

When Travis reached his apartment door, he didn't even try the key. He just knocked

and called that it was him, assuming Celeste
had both the chain and bar in place.

A few seconds later, the sounds of her
opening up told him he'd been right. However, he could hardly credit himself with a
brilliant deduction. Not when her life was in
danger.

She opened the door and the smell of something cooking wafted into the hall.

"Lasagna?" he guessed, stepping inside.

"Uh-huh. It was all I could find enough
ingredients for."

"Smells wonderful."

She smiled one of her terrific smiles, then
followed him into the living room and just
stood gazing expectantly at him as he took off
his jacket. It made him feel like a total failure.

"Nothing yet," he said as casually as he
could. "Maybe we'll get a break tomorrow."

The gun he'd shown her how to use was sitting on the coffee table, and as he was speaking her glance flickered to it—telling him
how worried she still was.

It made him want to wrap his arms around
her and assure her again that everything was
going to be just fine. But if he did, if she was
snuggled all soft and warm against him…

Uh-uh, forget that idea. Last night, she

couldn't have been more clear. She wanted him to keep his distance. And on top of that, she wasn't even sure how she felt about him.

"You look beat," she said. "And I barely put the lasagna in, so does a soda sound good?"

"Yeah, thanks, sounds great."

As she started for the kitchen, his thoughts turned back to the disconcerting fact that she didn't really know how she felt.

Oh, she'd *said* she liked him. And was attracted to him. But whether it was a tired phrase or not, actions spoke louder than words. And her actions had told him…actually, some of her words had, too.

One thing she'd said had been nagging at him all day. She wanted to wait until this *situation* was resolved, *then* see how they felt about each other.

Well, he didn't need to wait to know how *he* felt. He could remind himself about "slowly" and "carefully" from now till next year, but it wouldn't change the fact that he already knew he wanted a relationship with her.

Unfortunately, she couldn't say the same. So if she wanted him to keep his distance, he would. And not only because it was what *she* wanted.

He suspected he'd already fallen far too

hard for his own good. And if his feelings progressed even further, then she decided the two of them added up to a mistake, he'd find himself in the ranks of the walking wounded—which was not where he had any desire to be.

"I've been wanting to call and check my answering machine," she said, reappearing with two sodas and a glass for herself. "But I remembered you told me to only use your cell," she added as he popped the tabs on the cans.

After handing her one, he dug the phone out of his pocket and gave her that, as well. Then, while she pressed in the numbers, he waved Snoops off his recliner so he could sit down.

The cat graced him with an evil look before stalking out of the room, his tail straight in the air.

"Good thing I checked," Celeste said, the phone to her ear. "There's a message from an editorial coordinator about a project she wants me to work on next month. I'll have to get back to her in the morning."

He nodded, glad to hear she figured she'd still be alive next month, then took a slug of cola. The cold liquid felt good going down.

"And a friend called," she was saying.

He nodded again.

"Oh, no," she whispered a few seconds later.

"What?" he demanded, shooting to his feet.

She held up her hand, silencing him, and continued listening to a message that went on forever.

He took another swallow of cola, growing more impatient with each passing second.

"Oh, no," she said at last. "Travis, you've got to hear this for yourself."

CHAPTER TEN

Thursday, October 7, 7:12 p.m.

"Okay, I've got the messages replaying," Celeste said, handing Travis the phone.

He heard a beep and an older woman's voice said, "Ms. Langley, my name is Carol Schoenberg. You don't know me, and I hope you won't think it's awful of me to impose on you, but I'm just so worried about my daughter that I'm trying everyone I can think of who might...

"I'm sorry, I guess I'm not exactly being coherent. But my daughter is Donna Schoenberg. She'd be Donna Rainfield to you. That's her stage name."

Donna Rainfield? Travis glanced at Celeste.

She nodded, as if she knew exactly where the message had gotten to and was assuring him that yes, Donna Rainfield *was* the woman living with Bryce.

"I'm calling," the woman continued, "because she's disappeared and I'm afraid something awful's happened to her. And she told me Bryce phoned you, just the other day, after he heard about your brother…

"I'm very sorry about him. A horrible thing to have happened."

There was a pause, as if the woman was trying to think of something more to say about Parker but couldn't. Then she said, "At any rate, I thought you might have been talking to Bryce again. If you were, and if he said anything about Donna…

"I know you might not want to speak to me, but I'm hoping you'll call back. I've phoned the police, but they said there's nothing they can do for at least twenty-four hours. And I'm *sure* something's terribly wrong.

"Donna would never have just taken off without letting me know what was happening. So…well, my number is 555-6896. And I'd be *really* grateful if you'd call. So…please do. Bye."

Travis jotted down the number, then looked at Celeste.

"I've never even met Donna, let alone her mother," she said. "Why would she phone me, of all people?"

"Well, maybe she actually *was* trying everyone she could think of. And since she knew Bryce called you, maybe she *did* figure you'd talked to him again."

"I heard two *maybes*," Celeste said. "You don't think it's as straightforward as that?"

"What I think is that might not have been Donna's mother at all. It could have just been someone Bryce got to phone you."

"You've lost me."

"Celeste, if he *is* the one behind the contract, that call could have been an attempt to flush you out. Because the Ice Man's discovered that you're gone from your apartment."

CELESTE SAT on the couch beside Travis, anxiously waiting as he checked the phone book—while Snoops eyed them from the recliner.

He'd selected it as "his" spot, and although she was glad he'd started to settle in she'd be happier if he hadn't decided to appropriate Travis's favorite chair. That was hardly purrfect houseguest behavior.

"It's listed," Travis said, his finger stopping halfway down a column. "C. Schoenberg. 555-6896. That's the number, isn't it?"

"Yes."

"Okay, then she's who she said she is. That leaves us with the question of whether she's legitimately worried about Donna or helping Bryce try to track you down."

"Which do you think?"

"My guess would be legit. If he *is* trying to find you, I doubt he'd involve his girlfriend's mother. But you never know, so let's return her call and see where it gets us."

"You mean *me* return her call," she said, not at all eager to talk to Donna Rainfield's mother.

When Travis shot her a smile, it made her wish they'd had more to smile about since they'd met. It also started her wondering—for about the thousandth time—whether she'd have kissed him again if the circumstances had been different.

Of course, if the circumstances had been different, she wouldn't be staying here with him.

"Aren't you the one who said she didn't want Hank and me doing everything?" he was asking.

She nodded. "I'll call her right now."

"Good, because my impersonation of a woman's voice is pretty awful."

"Well, your voice *is* a little on the deep side. But what do I say?"

"You'll have to play it by ear. She's obviously a talker, though, so with any luck it'll just be a matter of letting her talk.

"Oh, and there's no way she should even suspect you're not phoning from home. Not unless Bryce *did* put her up to calling. So if she asks about the number being different, tell her you're using your cell. Then end the conversation fast."

The cordless and Travis's cell were both sitting on the coffee table, but it was the cell phone he reached for.

And, of course, Mrs. Schoenberg might have caller ID. So just in case she *was* in cahoots with Bryce…

Just in case. Man, by this point she was well on the way to believing that her estranged husband actually was behind the contract. Because as hard as she found that to accept, if it wasn't him, then who was it?

"We're going to do a conference call," Travis said, pressing in a phone number. "Not that I'll say anything, but I want to listen. And if I hear something I think you should jump on, I'll signal you, okay?"

"Okay."

A second later, the cordless began ringing.

"That's me," Travis said, motioning her to answer.

Once she had, he said, "Now we'll add Mrs. Schoenberg."

He punched in a series of numbers and got a connection.

"You're on," he whispered.

She barely had time to lick her dry lips before a woman picked up.

"Mrs. Schoenberg?" she said.

"Yes?"

"This is Celeste Langley returning your call."

"Oh, thank you! I was hoping you'd get back to me. You're the only one I could think of who knows Bryce. Aside from Donna, I mean. And I'm just so frantic about her."

"You still haven't heard from her, then."

"No, and…Celeste, is it all right if I call you that?"

"Yes, it's fine."

"Good. Then…Celeste, when I explain why I'm so worried you'll tell me what you make of things? Honestly, I mean?"

"Yes, of course," she said, although she couldn't help thinking that making a promise to Donna's mother was pretty bizarre.

"Good, because if anyone knows Bryce it has to be you. And when I called the police they wouldn't even agree to send someone to question him."

"Question him?" she repeated. Travis was signaling she should jump on that, but she hardly needed prompting.

"Yes. They said they couldn't even consider Donna a missing person until twenty-four hours had passed, let alone start investigating her disappearance. But...I...oh, this is very awkward when I have no idea why your marriage ended. What happened between you and Bryce, I mean."

She almost rolled her eyes. *Donna* was what happened. She'd been the precipitating factor, at least.

"But...Celeste, I'm terrified that Bryce has killed my daughter."

"What?" she whispered, feeling as if the air had suddenly been sucked from her lungs.

When she looked at Travis, he mouthed, *You're doing great!*

She swallowed hard, certainly not feeling great. "Mrs. Schoenberg," she managed to say, "what on earth would make you think that Bryce..."

"Should I tell you the whole story?"

"Yes. Please."

"All right." She paused for a moment, then began. "Donna's in a play that closes this weekend. Just a not-much, off-Broadway thing at the Winslow Lane Theater, down in the Village.

"But she had an audition this morning for another role. Still off-Broadway, but a bigger part. She was very excited about it.

"Then, a little before noon, her agent phoned me—trying to find her because she hadn't shown up. And that isn't like Donna. Her career's terribly important to her, so she's always very reliable.

"At any rate, he'd already called her apartment, but I thought, well maybe she was in the shower or something, so I tried."

"And she wasn't there," Celeste said.

"No, so then I phoned Bryce at his office. And he told me they'd had a fight last night and broken up. That didn't surprise me. The fight didn't, I mean. Because Donna called me yesterday afternoon to see what I thought about…

"Well, Bryce told her he intends to go to the service for your brother. And Donna didn't like that idea. She's always been afraid you and Bryce will get back together."

"We won't," she said, glancing at Travis to find he was watching her.

"Maybe not, but Donna isn't so sure. Some of the things Bryce does… She wanted them to get a new apartment, for example. Didn't want to be living where he'd lived with you. Felt as if she was just temporarily filling in for you. But he refused to even discuss it and…

"I've gotten off track, though. The point is that he told me they had a fight and he ordered her to get out. Said he wanted her gone by the time he got home from work today.

"And when I mentioned the audition he said she'd probably just forgotten about it because she was upset. But I didn't buy that.

"When she's upset, she calls me. Like she did yesterday. She's my only child and we've always been close."

"I see," Celeste murmured, glancing at Travis again.

This time, he gave her an encouraging nod.

"That's why the fact that I hadn't heard from her…well, I was certain something awful must have happened. So I went to their building and convinced the concierge he had to unlock the apartment. Told him Donna must be dreadfully sick or something. And…"

"Mrs. Schoenberg?" Celeste said when the woman began to cry. "Mrs. Schoenberg, try to calm down and tell me the rest."

She sniffed a few times, then said, "There was no sign of Donna, but her clothes were still in the closet and the place was a disaster. Chairs overturned and stuff broken. They must have been throwing things at each other. And when I saw...well, that's when I called the police."

As she sniffed again, Travis whispered, "Ask if there was any blood."

Celeste grimaced, then said, "Was there anything else? I mean, anything else you could tell them except that she was gone and the place was a disaster?"

"No, but I thought they'd at least come and have a look. They didn't, though. They just said that if no one heard from her in the next twenty-four hours they'd take a missing-person report if I wanted.

"*If I wanted.* Can you imagine? After I'd told them he might have killed her?

"Anyway, just before you phoned I called the theater. And she isn't there. The curtain's at eight, so if she's not there by now...

"And twenty-four hours won't be up until tomorrow afternoon. By then, if Bryce *did*...

Celeste, what do you think? Would he…" The woman started crying again.

"Mrs. Schoenberg," she said quietly, "it sounds as if he and Donna had quite a row, but Bryce isn't a violent man. He was never abusive to me, so—"

"Then where is she? Why did she miss that audition? And her performance tonight? And why hasn't she at least phoned me?"

"I don't know," Celeste admitted as Travis moved closer and mouthed, *Get Hank involved. I want him to hear this firsthand.*

She thought rapidly, then said, "Look, I've got an idea. A couple of homicide detectives came to see me after my brother was killed. They were very nice, and maybe if I called one of them he'd talk to you tonight."

"Really? You think?"

"Well, if you'd like, I'll see if I can get hold of either of them."

"Oh, please. I'd *really* appreciate that."

"All right, then, I'll give it a shot. And you try not to worry. Donna's probably just at a friend's place, too upset to go onstage tonight."

"No, she would have called. That's what has me so frightened."

"Well…I'll phone one of those detectives

as soon as we hang up. And either I'll get back to you or he'll call you."

"Oh, this is *so* kind of you. I'm hanging up right now. Bye."

"Bye."

Celeste clicked off, then said, "Will Hank still be on duty this late?"

"Uh-huh. Officially, we're on...I mean *he's* on the four-to-midnight shift this week. It was just that with your brother's murder we wanted to get a lot done right away, so the official shift went by the boards. He'll have a month's worth of overtime before he's done."

"And that's when his wife gets to see him?"

"It used to be. He's been divorced for a while now."

"That's too bad," she murmured. "Are there children involved?"

"One. A little boy. Jane walked out on both of them, so Hank has custody."

"Really."

She knew it happened, yet she still found it difficult to imagine a woman willingly giving up her child.

"How does he cope? What with the shift work and all, I mean."

"He's got a terrific housekeeper. She lives

in and doesn't seem to mind his hours. If it wasn't for her, I don't know what he'd do."

Celeste nodded, turning her thoughts back to Mrs. Schoenberg. "What about Donna's mother?" she said. "Did you get the impression she really *does* believe Donna's dead?"

"It sure sounded like it."

"Poor woman."

"At least she should feel better after Hank talks to her." Travis picked up his phone again and hit the speed dial for his partner's cell.

Roughly twenty-four hours had gone by since he'd told Hank about Bryce Wayland being Celeste's beneficiary. Which meant that at this point, Hank had probably learned more about the guy than his best friends knew. But he wouldn't have this hot-off-the-press news flash.

"Ballantyne," he answered.

"Got an interesting new development," Travis said, and proceeded to fill him in.

After that, Hank asked a couple of questions, then said he'd call Mrs. Schoenberg. Pronto.

"You'll get back to us tonight?"

"You bet."

"Talk to you later, then."

Travis clicked off, telling himself he was

doing as much as he could. But Carol Schoenberg would give Hank the perfect opening to pay Bryce Wayland a visit. And Travis was dying to go along.

However, that just wasn't an option. Aside from anything else, now that he was involved with Celeste he absolutely had to stay in the background.

He glanced at her, thinking *involved* wasn't actually the right word. It was where he'd figured they'd been heading, but since she'd laid down her ground rules he wasn't sure.

All he knew was that wherever they *did* go from here would be up to her. Regardless of the way he felt about her, he had no intention of kissing her again. If there was going to be a next move, it would have to be hers.

"Will Hank call her right away?" she asked.

"I'll bet he's already talking to her. And driving toward Bryce's at the same time. So if he *did* kill Donna—"

"Travis, I was telling her mother the truth. He's not a violent man. I mean, I've reached the stage of accepting that he might be behind the contract. But only because we can't think of who else it could be. And the idea of him actually killing Donna…"

Travis was tempted to point out that if

Bryce had murdered Steve it wouldn't be much of a surprise if he'd killed Donna, as well. He kept quiet, though, assuming she'd put that together for herself.

She did. Almost immediately.

"Yet there has to be *some* explanation for her disappearance," she continued slowly. "And if it *was* him who shot Steve, and Donna knew about it… Why on earth would he tell her, though?"

"I doubt he would have. But when you live with someone… It could have been as simple as her noticing blood on his clothes and getting the truth out of him.

"And once she knew what he'd done… The next time they have a major fight she threatens to tell. So he kills her. If he's already committed one murder, he's got more to lose by letting her talk than by getting rid of her."

After a few moments of silence, Celeste murmured, "Do you have any idea what it's like to think your husband—estranged or not—might be a murderer?"

"I can imagine," he said softly.

It was obviously a very unsettling thought. Unsettling enough, no doubt, to make her seriously wonder about her judgment in men.

So maybe he shouldn't be taking her rejection quite so personally.

But he found it impossible not to.

"Celeste?" he said after another silence. "Ever since we learned about that contract, the prospect of your going to the service for your brother has been worrying me. And now, with Mrs. Schoenberg saying Bryce will be there…"

She gazed at him for a minute, then said, "If Bryce is behind the contract, he isn't intending to kill me himself."

"No, but…"

"You're thinking the Ice Man might be there?"

"I'm just thinking we don't want to take the slightest chance."

"But you said a hit man never chooses a public place. A place where there'd be witnesses."

"Yeah, I did." And it was true. Usually.

Now that she was staying here, though, the Ice Man wouldn't know where to find her. So what if he figured the service could be his only chance at her—and decided to risk a public place?

"Travis, I can't *not* go."

He'd been certain she'd say that, which was

why he hadn't bothered raising the issue before this. But being right didn't make him any happier.

"Then maybe you could stay out of sight," he suggested. "There's probably some sort of special room for the family, or—"

"No," she interrupted. "Even though Steve and I weren't close, he was my brother. And I've got to be there for him."

"Celeste…"

She shook her head. "Not showing my face just isn't something I could do. I'd never be able to come to terms with it. Besides, you told me homicide detectives would be checking out the mourners. This Ice Man will realize that, won't he? And that will *ensure* he stays away."

"Probably," he admitted. But he wasn't going to let this drop until they'd reached some sort of compromise.

"You intend to go with your aunt?" he said.

"Yes. And my cousins. The funeral people said they'd send a car to pick them up, then come by my place."

"Instead of that, how about going with Hank?"

"My aunt would think it was awfully

strange. A man I've never even mentioned before."

"We can come up with an explanation. That it's standard procedure in a murder case. Or that you knew him long before he was assigned the case. Deciding on something believable won't be a problem."

"Then I guess it would make sense to have him with me."

"Good, because as much as I'd like it to be *me* with you, I just—"

"I know. You explained before. You'd be in hot water if—"

"No, it isn't that anymore. That was only when you were a suspect."

"Then…?"

"Nobody except Hank knows you're staying with me, and we want to keep it that way. So it wouldn't be a good idea for me to be sitting right beside you. Just in case."

Celeste gazed at him for a long moment, then said, "You're not one hundred percent sure the Ice Man won't be there, are you?"

"I'm ninety-nine percent sure. But why take any chances."

Especially when they were talking about her life.

By TEN O'CLOCK, Celeste was willing the phone to ring. Either of the phones, just as long as Hank was the one calling.

At Travis's suggestion, she'd rechecked her answering machine an hour ago. And sure enough, there'd been a second message from Donna's mother—thanking her for having Detective Ballantyne phone and telling her that he'd promised to pay Bryce a visit tonight.

But Hank hadn't gotten back to them yet, and she was dying to know where things stood.

If it *was* Bryce who wanted her dead, the sooner they were sure of that the better. Then Travis could make him call off the contract and she'd be able to get on with her life.

Her glance flickered to her own personal detective, and she couldn't help wondering what would happen to *them* after this was over. She'd hurt his feelings last night, maybe badly enough to make him reevaluate his—

"The news or an old episode of *Frasier?*" he said as a newscast began.

"The news is fine," she told him.

"You don't think Snoops would rather watch Eddie?"

She smiled. "If Eddie were a bird, he'd be all for it. But he doesn't like dogs."

"No?"

"Uh-uh. It's a genetic thing."

"That true?" he asked Snoops.

His question made her smile again.

Whereas Bryce had barely tolerated Snoops, Travis and the cat were already developing a rapport. They'd even reached a compromise in their battle for the recliner. Travis had possession, but Snoops was curled up on his lap.

She watched them for a minute, remembering how, last night, *she'd* been curled up with him. Right here on this couch.

Not tonight, though. After they'd eaten dinner and done the dishes, he'd headed straight for the chair.

But what had she expected? She'd told him she wanted to put things between them on hold, and he'd clearly taken that to heart.

The problem was, she kept suspecting she'd made a mistake. Because every time she looked at him she had trouble thinking of anything except how warm and safe she'd felt in his arms. And how his kiss had left her longing for more.

She was unsuccessfully trying to refocus

her thoughts when the phone finally rang. The sound made her jump.

Travis answered, then said, "Sure, see you in a minute.

"Hank," he told her, clicking off. "He's practically here, so I'll go let him in."

Snoops meowed a protest at being deposited on the floor, then leaped back onto the recliner the instant Travis started for the door.

In only a couple of minutes he was back, Hank on his heels.

As they sat down, Travis in the chair once more, Hank next to her on the couch, Travis said, "So what's the story? Is Bryce our guy?"

"Hard to say," Hank told him. "Once he recovered from the shock of a detective showing up at his door, he was pretty cool. The only serious reaction I got was when I told him Donna's mother had called the police—and suggested he'd murdered her. That really browned him off."

"But it would have whether he's guilty or not," Travis said.

"Does he know it was *me* who suggested you talk to Mrs. Schoenberg?" Celeste asked.

"Uh-uh. I just said she'd called us and I'd ended up talking to her."

That didn't mean, however, that Bryce

wouldn't eventually hear about her involvement. And if he did, he sure wouldn't be happy. But that was nowhere near the top of her "things to worry about" list.

"Did you tell him you were Homicide?" Travis was asking.

Hank grinned. "I just said NYPD detective. Thought I'd save the homicide bit for next time.

"At any rate, he gave me the same version of what happened as he gave Mrs. Schoenberg. He and Donna had a fight. He said he wanted her gone by the time he got home from work today and she was. End of story."

"Did you ask if she'd taken her things?"

Hank nodded. "He said she hadn't. In fact, he didn't say anything that I knew was a lie. But he didn't volunteer anything, either, and when I hit him with the bit about the apartment having been a disaster he got pretty perturbed. He'd straightened everything up, and nobody'd told him that Mrs. Schoenberg had been there.

"But he swore the apartment was fine when he left for his office this morning— that throwing things around was just Donna's way of expressing her anger before she left."

"Did he have any idea where she might be?" Celeste asked.

"Not that he was telling me. His theory was that she's simply dropped out of sight to get people worried. Make it look as if he might have driven her to suicide or something. He basically said she's a fruitcake, so nothing she did would surprise him.

"Do you know if she actually is nutsy?" he added to Celeste.

She shook her head. "But if she is, Bryce couldn't have realized it until after she moved in with him. He's not a fool."

Travis and Hank exchanged a glance she couldn't read, then Travis said, "Where are you going from here?"

"Well, unless Donna turns up, her mother will file a missing person's tomorrow. So there's a chance we could get a warrant to search his apartment."

"Not *much* of a chance."

"Why not?" Celeste asked.

"Because women are always having fights with their boyfriends, then disappearing," Travis explained. "And they normally turn up safe and sound. Which means it's unlikely any judge would issue a warrant to search the apartment of a respectable citizen—a lawyer yet—just because Donna's mother is worried about her."

When she turned to Hank, he nodded his agreement. Then, before she could ask anything more, Travis's cell began ringing.

"Quinn," he answered.

After a brief pause, he said, "Yes, Mr. Reese, of course I remember you."

Reese? Evan Reese? She glanced at her watch, wondering what on earth the man wanted at all, let alone this late at night.

Then she looked at Travis once more, as he said, "A favor? What sort of favor?"

CHAPTER ELEVEN

Thursday, October 7, 10:52 p.m.

TRAVIS WAITED FOR Evan Reese to elaborate, wondering what he was up to and wishing he could put the man on speakerphone so Celeste and Hank could listen in.

Saying they were curious would be a distinct understatement. They were leaning far enough forward on the couch that they were at risk of tipping off.

"It involves Celeste Langley," Reese finally announced.

That was *not* something Travis wanted to hear. He exhaled slowly, then looked meaningfully over at the others and said, "A favor involving Celeste Langley?"

The words were barely out before he regretted them. They'd clearly heightened Celeste's anxiety level—so much so that he decided he wouldn't try to fill in any more blanks until after the call was finished.

"Yes, I need to talk to her," Reese was saying. "But every time I've phoned I've gotten her machine."

Travis fumed. Both he and Hank had made it clear that Reese wasn't to contact Celeste again, yet the guy couldn't care less.

"I think she's home but screening her calls," Reese continued. "She'll pick up for *you,* though, won't she?"

When Travis simply let that pass, Reese said, "I never leave messages on machines. It's a matter of principle. So I've been sitting here looking at your card, and thinking that if you wouldn't mind just asking her to phone me…"

"Mr. Reese, the last I heard, Ms. Langley didn't want to—"

"No, you don't understand. I've learned something about her brother's death. Something very important."

Travis could feel adrenaline racing through his veins.

He doubted Reese had learned anything that Hank and the rest of the detectives weren't already on top of. But it was conceivable that all along he'd known something they didn't.

Even though he had an airtight alibi for

the evening Steve Parker was murdered, that didn't rule out the possibility he'd played a role in the killing.

"Something very important," Travis repeated evenly. "In that case, you should be talking to Detective Ballantyne. He's in charge of the case, so why don't I have *him* call you, and—"

"No. I'm not going to discuss it with anyone except Celeste. Not initially. After I've talked to her, I'll be ready for Ballantyne. But I've got to talk to her first."

"Why?"

"Because I want her to know it's *me* who's giving you people her brother's murderer."

"Mr. Reese, you have my word that she'll know you're helping."

"I'm talking about more than *helping*," he snapped. "Didn't you hear me? I can give you the murderer."

"Well, that's absolutely terrific. But having you talk to her first just isn't the way we work. So—"

"I talk to her first or I don't talk to anyone. Your decision." With that, he hung up.

"What?" Hank said the instant Travis clicked off.

"He says he knows who killed Steve Parker.

But he wants to tell Celeste before he'll talk to you. He wants her to call him."

"You have his number?" she asked.

"Wait a minute. Let's not forget this guy's a nut bar. He might not know a thing."

"On the other hand, he might," Hank said. "And there's only one way to find out. I've got his number right here," he added, digging his notebook from his pocket.

"Yeah, I guess you're right," Travis muttered.

But that hardly meant he liked the idea of Celeste phoning Reese. Both times she'd spoken to him before, he'd scared the devil out of her.

"Let's wait until morning," he suggested. "We don't want to seem too eager about giving in to him."

"We don't want him having time to change his mind, either," Hank pointed out.

"Yeah...well...okay, but we'll do the conference call routine again."

Once they had their two cell phones and the apartment's line linked, Hank punched in the numbers that would add Reese to the mix.

"Are you sure you're up to this?" Travis asked Celeste.

She nodded, although she looked awfully nervous.

When Reese answered on the first ring, an image of a vulture hovering over a phone popped into Travis's mind.

"Mr. Reese, it's Celeste Langley," she said. "Detective Quinn just called and asked me to phone you. I hope it's not too late."

"No, not at all. I'm a night owl."

Or a night vulture, as the case may be.

Reese said nothing more, so Hank gestured for Celeste to pick up the ball.

"Detective Quinn said you wanted to talk to me about my brother's case," she prompted.

"Yes, I do. Are you free for lunch tomorrow?"

She shot Travis an anxious glance; he firmly shook his head. There was no way she was getting together with that weirdo.

"I was thinking Joe Allen. On Forty-sixth. You know? Near Eighth?"

"Ah...well, yes, I know where it is, but I got the impression that you only wanted to talk on the phone."

"No. Detective Quinn must have misunderstood."

"I guess he must have. But I'm afraid I'm

not up to socializing. I'm still feeling pretty shaky about the murder, and—"

"I understand. This won't be socializing, though. And it really isn't something we can discuss over the phone."

"But—"

"Celeste, I know who killed your brother. And I want to see your face when I tell you."

She looked at Travis once more, a question in her eyes.

He mouthed, *I'm not sure.* Reese was probably lying. But possibly, he wasn't.

"Well…that's wonderful. Your knowing, I mean. It'll be such a relief when the case is closed. Still, I think it would be more appropriate for—"

"Joe Allen. Tomorrow at one. I've already made the reservation," Reese added. Then the connection was broken.

"Call him back," Travis told her. "Tell him you won't be there and see if you can—"

"Hey," Hank interrupted. "Let's not be too hasty. None of us wants her face-to-face with Reese, but what if he really *does* know who our perp is?"

"I'll go," Celeste said. "Hank's right. I have to. He might really know."

"But…" Travis eyed her for a minute, then

simply shook his head and didn't bother with the rest.

Her expression said he could argue against her decision till one tomorrow afternoon without changing her mind.

BEING ON LEAVE, and not exactly in the CO's good books, Travis wasn't about to go anywhere near Manhattan North Homicide. But he'd wanted a couple of things, so he'd asked Hank to pick them up.

Hank dropped them off a little after eleven in the morning, which left plenty of time.

"Everything else organized?" Travis asked, reaching for the bag.

"Uh-huh. A couple of our guys will be having lunch in the restaurant. Two more will be in a car near the entrance. And I'm putting a uniform in the alley out back."

"Great. Thanks."

"Hey, no thanks necessary. I don't want anything happening to her, either. But Reese isn't likely to try much in a restaurant. You know that. And with any luck he *can* tell us who killed Parker."

"Yeah, maybe he can," Travis agreed, although he really doubted it. The idea of him handing them their perp seemed just too improbable.

"I'll stop by again later," Hank said as they walked over to where he'd double-parked. "I want to hear the details firsthand."

"Yeah. Sure." Travis waited until Hank had climbed into his car, before starting back to the apartment. When he got there, Celeste glanced curiously at the bag.

"Just a couple of things for your meeting with Reese," he said.

She eyed him for a minute, then said, "You're really worried about it, aren't you."

Admitting she was right would only make *her* more anxious, so he merely said, "I just don't want to take any chances, and we're not going to. For starters, you won't be meeting him at *his* location. I'll be the one at Joe Allen. I'll bring him to you."

"And I'll be…?"

"Down the block at another restaurant called Zia's."

"What if he doesn't go for the change of venue?"

"Then he doesn't get to talk to you."

"But—"

"Celeste, I'm not letting him have control. And if that means he takes a hike, then we do without whatever he has to say. But if he plays along, we want a place where keeping you under surveillance will be easy."

"Surveillance?"

"Yeah, we'll have some of our people at Zia's. It's small. Easy to see who's doing what."

"Travis…do you actually think Reese might…" She paused, glancing over to where his gun was sitting.

"You won't need a gun," he told her. And surely that was true.

As Hank had said, even a nut bar like Reese wouldn't likely try much in a restaurant. And if he did, their fellows would take care of him. Fast.

Besides, Celeste had never used a gun. If she tried to, she'd be lucky to remember half of what he'd shown her the other night. And he knew of more than one instance where someone inexperienced had ended up with his gun being used against him.

"You'll be wearing a wire," he continued. "So if there's any trouble, I'll hear it the moment it starts."

"A wire," she repeated, looking surprised. And uneasy.

"It's just another precaution," he told her.

"As I said, we're not taking any chances. So let's get the transmitter taped to you."

"You mean taped to my skin?"

When he nodded, she said, "Isn't there some other way?"

"Uh-uh. If it can shift around we either get static or lose the sound entirely."

She said nothing more, so he took the mike and a roll of tape from the bag and hunkered down in front of her, swallowing hard as he inhaled her perfume.

"Okay," he said as nonchalantly as he could. "If you just pull your sweater up a few inches..."

She did, revealing an expanse of creamy skin.

Swallowing hard again, he ripped a length of tape from the role.

"That's going to hurt when it comes off, isn't it," she murmured.

He looked up. "Yeah, 'fraid so. But it won't be too bad."

"No, I know. I'm just a chicken. I've always had sort of a...thing about pulling off tape. Even a tiny bandage. I realize it's childish, but..."

When she substituted a little shrug in place of the rest of her explanation, he almost asked if she thought she could manage this job herself. But he had to be sure it was done right, so he reached for the transmitter and rested it against her chest.

Her skin felt as warm and smooth as sundrenched silk; he had an almost overwhelming urge to caress it. Somehow, he forced himself to resist.

He secured the top of the device with the strip of tape, trying not to breathe in any more of her perfume.

"Hold that in place while I get another piece," he said.

After ripping off a second length of tape, he fixed the bottom of the transmitter to her rib cage.

"That's got it," he said, standing up. "Now, all you have to do is clip the mike to your bra. About the center would be good."

He didn't watch her fiddle under her sweater with the mike. Instead, he stared straight at the wall and took four times as long as necessary to tuck the receiver into his ear.

"Okay, we'll do a final volume-level test when you're ready to go," he said at last. "But right now I just want to make sure everything's working okay.

"I'll go out into the hall and close the door. And you start speaking quietly. The way you would sitting in a restaurant."

"Where will you be then? When I'm actually in the restaurant, I mean."

"I'll have to scope things out once we get there, but probably in the alley. On the street, the noise of the traffic could be a problem."

"Right," Celeste murmured, not taking her eyes off him as he turned and started for the door.

She had a suspicion that even if she tried to it would prove impossible.

She'd barely been able to breathe while he'd taped on the transmitter, barely been able to keep her hands from cradling his face and drawing him to his feet...from drawing his mouth to hers.

Knowing how expert his kisses were, how good they made her feel, she'd had to muster all the determination she could to keep her cool.

Cool? She slowly shook her head as the word echoed in her mind. There was absolutely nothing cool about her when she was as close to Travis Quinn as she'd just been.

The voice of common sense that kept warning her not to rush into anything, to wait and see how she felt about him after this was all over, was becoming so faint she could barely hear it over the sound of her heartbeat.

TRAVIS LEFT Celeste sitting at a table in Zia's and started down the block toward Joe Allen—telling himself, once again, that she'd be fine.

He'd seen the detectives parked outside, watching the street. And the ones inside, who'd be keeping a close eye on her.

Yes, his listening in on her conversation was going to be blatant overkill. But he just didn't want to take the slightest risk. If anything happened to her...

"Nothing will," he said under his breath.

He reached Joe Allen at a quarter to one, checked with the maître d' to make sure Reese hadn't arrived early, then waited outside the restaurant.

At five to, a taxi pulled up and Reese climbed out. The moment Travis spotted him, his gut tightened. If Reese did *anything* to try to harm Celeste, he'd kill him.

"Mr. Reese," he said as the man turned away from the cab.

"What are you doing here?" he demanded.

"There's been a slight change of plans. Ms. Langley would rather eat somewhere else."

"Then why didn't she say so last night?"

Travis shrugged. "She's waiting for you. At a restaurant right down the block," he added, gesturing in its direction.

"This is a *private* lunch," Reese snapped. "You're not invited."

"I've already eaten. So I'll just show you where—"

"I don't need a guide. What's the place called?"

"Zia's."

Reese wheeled away and started off.

Travis watched him for a few seconds, willing his blood pressure to drop back to normal, then headed rapidly in the opposite direction. He rounded the corner of Eighth and began to jog.

Earlier, when he'd checked to make sure that Pazzia's back door was unlocked, he'd introduced himself to the uniform posted in the alley. So this time he merely nodded to the guy, then stuck the receiver in his ear— just in time to hear Reese say, "Ms. Langley, I'm Evan Reese."

"It's nice to meet you," she said amid the noise of a chair scraping across the floor.

Travis wasn't sure whether she actually sounded nervous or it was only his imagination.

"You don't like Joe Allen?" Reese asked.

"Oh, no, it isn't that. I just knew I'd feel more relaxed here. It's one of my favorite places. I come in all the time, and I thought, since it was just down the street, you wouldn't mind."

"I don't. This looks fine."

"Good. I know it was presumptuous of me, but I'm not very comfortable about meeting strangers, so I decided… I'm babbling, aren't I. That's one of the dumb things I do when I first meet someone."

"Don't worry about it. We won't be strangers for long."

There was a silence, then she said, "I could hardly sleep after we talked last night. Just couldn't stop thinking that once you tell the police who killed Steve they'll be able to wrap up the case. But it was thoughtful of you to want to tell me first. So…the suspense is killing me."

He could picture the gorgeous smile she was giving Reese, and the image made him clench his hands. He didn't want the woman he loved having to force smiles for a creep like that.

The woman he loved.

The realization he'd gotten to that stage hit him like a proverbial bolt from the blue.

Oh, he'd been aware, for days now, that he didn't want *them* to end when this was over. Aware he wanted enough time to find out how they'd be together under *normal* circumstances. But the fact that, without even noticing, he'd crossed the emotional line and fallen in love with her...

How could he possibly have let that happen?

He ordered himself to put the question out of his mind for the moment, because Reese had started speaking again.

"Before we get to who killed your brother," he was saying, "there's something else I want to discuss."

Travis clenched his fists. He was already sensing that Reese had no intention of playing straight.

"Oh?" Celeste said. "What?"

"I was very close to him. I mean, I know all about transference between a patient and his psychiatrist, but I'm talking more than that.

"There was something unique between us. A bond. An incredibly strong thread of communality.

"Now that he's gone, I feel as if there's an emptiness in my life that I have to fill. And I keep thinking...

"Remember what we discussed on the phone that first time? The cosmic connection between us? You, an editor. Me, a writer. You, Steve's sister. Me, having a special relationship with him.

"It's like the 'six degrees of separation' thing. But with you and me there was only one degree. Your brother.

"With him gone there shouldn't even be one. I guess there already isn't, since we're here together. And...Celeste, I want to be your friend. I want—"

"Mr. Reese?"

"Evan. Please call me Evan."

"Evan, then," she said slowly, *definitely* sounding nervous now.

Come on, Travis silently urged her. *You're doing fine.*

"As I explained last night," she continued, "I'm still pretty shaky, emotionally speaking. So it really would be better if...if we left talking about any relationship between us for another time."

"I see," Reese said icily.

Suddenly conscious of the fact that he still had his hands clenched, Travis uncurled his fingers, reminding himself two police detectives were sitting not ten feet from Celeste. But he wanted to be inside the restaurant himself. Right there at that table between her and Reese.

"Well, if you don't feel up to talking now," he said, "it'll have to wait for another time. Waiter?

"We won't be eating after all," he said a few seconds later. "But here's something for you."

The waiter thanked him. Then, after a pause, Celeste said, "Evan? What about my brother's killer?"

"What about him?"

"You were going to tell me who he is."

"Oh, yes, of course. I was. But you know, I've decided I don't feel like getting into that. So let's leave it for another time, too."

A chair scraped across the floor, that sound followed by faint, fading footsteps, then silence—until Celeste whispered, "Travis, he's just walked out the door."

CELESTE COULDN'T remember ever having been so utterly disappointed in herself. If only she'd said the right things to Evan Reese, if only…

On the other hand, maybe Travis was right. Maybe, regardless of what she'd said…

She didn't want to ask him yet again, but when he opened his apartment door she couldn't keep from saying, "You *really* don't think he knows who killed Steve?"

He gave her a weary smile. "No. Hank'll pay him another visit. Make absolutely sure. But I'm certain he just wanted to meet you. And he'd have said anything he thought would make you agree."

"But why would he want to meet me? Oh, stupid question. Because he's crazy. Because he's decided we're cosmically connected."

"Celeste…"

"What?"

"Nothing," he said, tossing his jacket onto the end of the couch.

She stood gazing at the gun in his shoulder holster, reminding herself that the meeting with Reese could have gone a lot worse than it had. At least he hadn't pulled a gun on her.

But her hopes had been so high, and if she'd just handled things better…

"Celeste, Reese *doesn't* know. Trust me on

that. So no matter what you said or did we still wouldn't have the name."

"Thanks, I needed that," she murmured, although she still had a horrible suspicion that Travis wasn't *entirely* certain, that he was only trying to make her feel better.

"Why don't you go take off that wire," he suggested. "I know how itchy the tape can get."

She nodded, then started for the bedroom.

Snoops, who was lying in the center of the bed, lazily watched her remove her blazer and sweater.

That done, she stood looking down at the securely taped listening device, telling herself she wasn't going to be a big baby about getting it off. She couldn't be, because if she was she'd have to ask Travis for help. And she was only too aware what a dangerous move that would be.

Tentatively, she tugged at one corner of the tape. Not even a millimeter came free. It only pulled her skin—which hurt.

"You're being absolutely ridiculous," she muttered, having a shot at a different corner. It hurt even more.

She ordered herself to just rip the strips off,

but she'd never in her entire life been able to go that route.

She didn't have a particularly low threshold for pain when it came to anything else. And she'd always known this was a stupid hang-up. But it had never made her feel like quite such an idiot before.

"Celeste?" Travis called. "You okay in there?"

"Fine, thanks. I'll just be another minute."

So what was she going to do? Live with a wire taped to her chest until the adhesive wore out?

She doubted that was even an option. Travis would have to return the transmitter long before then.

Annoyed with herself, she pulled her sweater back on and headed for the living room.

Travis had removed his gun and was sitting in his recliner, glancing through a magazine.

"I have a little problem," she told him.

"Oh?"

"I mentioned it before, remember? A thing about taking off bandages. I've always got to shut my eyes and have someone else yank them off while I'm not looking. And Snoops just isn't up to it."

Travis grinned. "I guess not having hands can be a real problem."

"Yes, well, being a chicken can be a real problem, too," she said, easing her sweater up a few inches.

CHAPTER TWELVE

Friday, October 8, 2:11 p.m.

THE MOMENT TRAVIS rose from the recliner, Celeste realized that asking for his help had been an even more dangerous idea than she'd been thinking.

His dark eyes were looking straight into her soul; and a smile played at the corners of his mouth as he crossed the room.

"So," he said, stopping in front of her. "You close your eyes and I yank away. That's the deal?"

"Unless you've got a pain-free method I've never heard of."

"'Fraid not," he said. "It *is* going to hurt a bit."

He waited, obviously expecting her to say something more, but the jumble of words in her head wasn't making the slightest sense.

And she knew why. The reason was standing not six inches from her.

She liked Travis Quinn. But she still didn't want to make a mistake. Still didn't want to take their relationship any further without being sure it was a wise thing to do.

He reached out and rested his fingers beside one end of the tape. She gasped, even though his touch was gentle.

"Hey," he said quietly, "it's not supposed to hurt until I pull."

"I...ah..."

She knew she must be positively radiating the message that she wanted him to kiss her. So why was he still just standing there?

Because *he'd* decided it wouldn't be a good idea? For all she knew he'd decided he didn't even like her.

A dozen second thoughts began racing through her mind, every one of them prompting her to say, "Travis...maybe we should just leave this for a while."

"And delay the inevitable?"

He gave her the biggest grin she'd ever seen, which left her uncertain whether he meant that pulling off the tape was inevitable or...

"Close your eyes and let's just do it," he said.

She closed her eyes. A second later, she yelped as he tore off the tape.

"Sorry," he said.

"No. No, it wasn't really that bad." And he'd pulled both strips at once. Thankfully.

"Sure you're okay?" He trailed his fingertips along where the bottom length of tape had been—making her skin tingle.

"Yes. I'm fine." Except that she felt as if she were melting inside.

After tossing the transmitter and the balled-up tape onto the couch, he simply stood gazing at her.

"Travis...I..."

"What?"

She had to decide. Now. And since she'd never before felt the way she felt about him... She loved him. How could it possibly be anything but love?

Taking a deep breath, she reached up and gently rested her hand on his jaw.

He drew a breath that was every bit as deep as hers, then murmured, "Celeste...the other night you said you didn't want to rush into anything."

"That was the other night," she whispered.

He smiled again, another slow, soft smile that did further devastating things to her insides. Then he swept her up in his arms and kissed her.

"You know how long I've been wanting to do this?" he whispered, his breath hot against her skin.

"No. How long?"

"From the first moment I saw you. I just wouldn't admit it to myself right away."

"Why not?"

"Because...does it really matter?"

"No," she murmured. Nothing mattered except the here and now. The two of them.

TRAVIS WANTED THE WORLD to stop turning, wanted everything in it to stay exactly this way for eternity. She had come to him. She recognized there was something special between them.

His wildest imaginings had been nothing compared with the reality of making love to Celeste. And now, lying with his sweat-slicked body curled around hers, a damp tendril of her hair tickling his neck, he knew he'd be happy to stay this way forever.

Happy? He couldn't stop himself from grinning. How about *deliriously* happy? Or wildly? Ridiculously? Incomparably?

"What?" she murmured, snuggling even more closely against him on the couch where they had settled.

"What, what?"

"I can feel you smiling."

"Yeah?"

"Uh-huh."

He nuzzled her shoulder. "You must be wrong. I can't smile and do that at the same time."

"Well, you *were* smiling."

"Yeah, I was," he admitted as she lifted her face face to him.

"Why?"

"Because of the way you make me feel."

That started *her* smiling. "How do I make you feel?"

"Oh, you know. Heart pounding like a jackhammer. Ten feet tall. Able to leap high buildings in a single bound. All the standard stuff."

"Standard for what?" she said, running her fingers through the hair at the back of his neck.

He took a deep breath. He'd never said the words, and the prospect of saying them made him feel as if he were balancing at the end of a mile-high diving board.

"Standard for being in love," he told her at last. "Or so I hear. It's never happened to me before."

"Really?"

"Yeah. Really."

"Oh, Travis. It's never happened to me before, either. Not like this. Not anywhere near like this."

His heart began hammering harder still. Now she had him thinking he could leap a hundred high buildings in a single bound. "Well...that's good, then, isn't it."

She kissed his chin. "If I were in editor mode, I'd change the *good* to *fantastic*."

He laughed. "Is that how it's going to be? Whenever I open my mouth, I'll be at risk of your editing what I say?"

"Mmm, it'll depend on what you say."

He was sorely tempted to say he wanted to be with her for the rest of his life. See if she edited that. But he didn't.

Even though it seemed as if he'd known her forever, in reality it hadn't been long. And there was still the major problem of that contract.

Until they got to the bottom of it, there'd always be the danger of the world suddenly crashing down around them. And he had to eliminate the chance it might before they could talk about the future.

He didn't consider himself a superstitious

man. He simply didn't believe in tempting fate.

"Travis?" Celeste murmured, looking so serious that he wondered if she'd been reading his mind.

"What?"

"I suddenly started thinking about Steve's service being tomorrow. And it seems so… us together like this when…"

"There's nothing wrong with us being together like this, Celeste. Nothing at all. People can't control when they fall in love."

He kissed her throat, then cuddled her closely once more and sat back. But now that she'd raised the subject of her brother's service, his concerns about it were front and center in his mind.

They were no closer to identifying the Ice Man than they'd been on day one. He wouldn't know the guy if they were standing in the same elevator. Or sitting in the same funeral home chapel, as the case may be.

And what if the lowlife *did* try to kill Celeste tomorrow?

It might be unlikely, but it wasn't out of the question—a fact that was still worrying him when his cell began ringing.

Too much of a cop to ignore it, he pulled

away from Celeste and headed into the kitchen.

"Quinn," he answered.

"It's me," Hank said. "I said I'd stop by, remember?"

"Right, of course," he lied. His head had been too full of concerns about Celeste to remember a thing.

"Good. I'll be there in two minutes."

"Yeah, okay." He put the phone down and strode rapidly back into the living room.

"Hank'll be here in a couple of minutes," he said. "He wants to hear about your meeting with Reese."

"Oh, man," Celeste murmured. "He seems to work twenty-five hours a day. We've got to find him another wife. Maybe then he'd go home more often."

Travis laughed, but her words reminded him why he'd always sworn he'd never get married. Although standing here gazing at her, still flushed from holding her... Well, he wouldn't be the first guy in the world to change his mind.

That thought rattling around in his head, he went downstairs to let Hank in. By the time he got back up to the apartment, Celeste was curled up on the couch, her nose in a book.

"So?" Hank said without preliminaries.

"I didn't do well," she told him.

"She did just fine," Travis said. "Reese was the problem, not her."

After they'd given Hank a detailed summary, he said, "I'll bet Travis is right. The creep doesn't know a thing. So let's forget him for the time being and talk about tomorrow.

"I'll pick you up here, Celeste, and be right beside you the entire time. I spoke to someone at the funeral home, and the family stays in a little anteroom until just before the service. I'll be in there with you. Plus, we'll have people in the chapel."

"What about her wearing a vest?" Travis said.

"You mean a bulletproof vest?" she asked.

He nodded.

"Not a good idea," Hank said.

"Why not?"

"Because this Ice Man probably checked her out as soon as he took on the contract. And she's thin enough that if he's seen her before he'd realize she was wearing one."

"Wait a minute," she said, her voice barely a whisper. "Do you actually figure he's going to be there? Travis and I talked about that, but…"

As her words trailed off and she shook her head, Travis shot Hank a glance to say he was scaring the wits out of her.

"No," he quickly said. "I *don't* figure he'll be there. I just don't want to rule out the possibility. Not completely, I mean."

"Listen for a sec," Travis said. "We're not really thinking he'd *try* anything there. We're just thinking he might have learned you're not staying in your apartment. And that if he has, he could be planning on finding out where you *are* staying by following you from the service."

"But—"

"We've got that covered," Hank interrupted her. "You don't have to worry about it.

"As for the vest," he continued, focusing on Travis once more, "if he *is* there, and it's obvious she's wearing one, he'll figure it's because we've heard about the contract. And that would make him a dozen times more careful."

"Or it might make him give up on the hit," Travis pointed out. And that would be the best thing in the entire world.

"Uh-uh, buddy. You're into wishful thinking. You know these guys. Every one of them is convinced he's smarter than we are. So, as I said, he sees a vest, it only makes him more careful. Which is the last thing we want.

"Oh, and by the way, I dropped in on Carol Schoenberg. Figured she might tell me something useful about Bryce."

"And did she?"

"Not really. She gave me a picture of Donna, though." He produced an eight-by-ten photograph from a folder and handed it to Travis. "One of her publicity shots."

Travis gazed at it, thinking Donna Rainfield was an extremely good-looking woman—somewhere in her twenties, with glossy dark hair and enormous eyes.

"May I see it?" Celeste asked.

When he handed it to her, she murmured, "She's beautiful, isn't she."

He wanted to say she wasn't nearly as beautiful as Celeste, but he'd save that until after Hank was gone.

THE MEMORIAL SERVICE was set for eleven in the morning; Hank arrived at Travis's apartment well before ten.

Celeste managed a smile for him—just

barely, though. She was both more upset and more frightened than she wanted to admit, which made smiling difficult.

Last night, she and Travis had done their best to pretend everything was fine in their little corner of the world. They'd ordered in Chinese and eaten it curled up on the couch while watching a movie.

But this morning the bright light of day had chased away her illusions. Things were about as far from "fine" as they could be.

"I saw Evan Reese again after I left here yesterday," Hank told her as Travis closed the door.

"And? *Does* he know who killed Steve?"

"No, I really don't think he's got a clue. He told me he'd only said he knew because he wanted to meet you, face-to-face. And he figured that would make you agree."

"Scuzzball," Travis muttered. "We should be charging him with something."

"What? Lying?" Hank said grimly.

"How about obstruction of justice? Or at the very least, public mischief."

"Yeah, well, let's not forget who his uncle Fred is. I don't think we want to do anything that could be construed as harassment."

Travis simply shook his head, his expression dark.

"Oh, and by the way, Celeste, I'm afraid he's going to be at the service."

"You're joking!" Travis said.

"Uh-uh. I told him I doubted she'd want him there, but it didn't do any good.

"He said it's a free world. And that it was only appropriate for him to go. That Parker wasn't just his psychiatrist. They were also close friends."

"In his dreams," Travis snapped. "But is everything else under control?"

When Hank nodded, Celeste looked at Travis once more.

He was watching her, a clear message in his dark eyes. As he'd told her yesterday, he wished *he* could be the one playing bodyguard.

That was what she wished, too, yet if they didn't want anyone to suspect she was staying here with him, they just couldn't risk being seen together.

She forced her gaze from his, telling herself that when this was all over they'd be able to be together—anywhere and everywhere—without worrying about who might see them and what they might think.

TRAVIS CHOSE A SEAT near the rear of the funeral home's chapel, so he'd have a good view of everyone coming in.

Only a few people had gotten there before him, and he recognized a couple of them as NYPD detectives. A man and a woman who were nonchalantly standing in separate places near the entrance, both looking expectant, as if waiting to meet someone.

Of course, Hank had assured him their people would be here. But actually spotting two of them started him breathing a little more easily.

No matter how many times he reminded himself the Ice Man would probably never try anything in a place like this, "probably" was no guarantee. And if he *did* come here…

Man, if he did show, wouldn't there be *something* that would tell them who he was?

Travis mentally shook his head, knowing that wasn't likely. The sleazoid would undoubtedly look like Everyman. And he'd be careful not to do anything that would make him stick out from the crowd.

But maybe, with luck… Travis forced himself to lean back and scan each newcomer.

As promised, Evan Reese eventually appeared. He stared straight at Travis without the slightest sign of recognition, then took a seat near the front.

Travis felt like going up there and checking the jerk for a concealed weapon just to upset him. However, common sense prevailed.

As Hank had said, they'd be stupid to do anything that could be construed as harassment. And he knew Reese wasn't the Ice Man. Nothing added up to that.

A few more people wandered in, among them Jill Flores and Beth Winston.

A couple of minutes later, Celeste's estranged husband appeared. Hank had given Travis a definitive description, so there was little doubt the man standing in the doorway was Bryce Wayland.

Not very tall, maybe five-foot-nine at the outside, yet a man most women would probably consider good-looking. His short brown hair was well styled, his dark-rimmed glasses lent him an aura of intelligence and his suit was expensive and definitely not off the rack.

Travis hated him on sight.

Well, actually, he'd been hating him for days now—ever since he'd realized it almost had to be Bryce who was behind that contract.

Pausing at the back of the chapel, Bryce

slowly checked out the gathering. Finally, he walked partway to the front and sat down beside an attractive woman he obviously knew.

A friend of Celeste's, Travis guessed. Another blonde, like her.

For a split second, he wondered if Bryce was one of those guys who had a thing about blondes. Then the photograph of Donna flashed into his mind. She was a brunette.

That picture in his head started him wondering whether she'd surfaced yet. But if Hank had heard anything new, he'd have mentioned it. And surely Mrs. Schoenberg would have let him know if her daughter had been in touch. So...

Travis sat gazing at Bryce Wayland's back, thinking that if Donna turned up dead his apartment was going to be swarming with cops. By then, though, it might be too late to find evidence that would incriminate him.

He briefly let his mind wander down that road, then warned himself that he was doing too much hypothesizing based on too little solid evidence.

Oh, he realized it was because he was involved with Celeste, because he so desperately wanted this case wrapped up. But having a reason didn't make it right. He knew better than to start considering things as facts until he was certain that was what they were.

Donna was missing. Fact. Donna was dead. Pure speculation. If, as Bryce had suggested to Hank, she was a few pages short of a script, she really might have vanished simply to make people wonder what had happened to her.

There was also a chance, he made himself admit, that he was wrong about Bryce being behind the contract. Not *much* of a chance. Still, until they had something more damning than merely the terms of Adele Langley's will...

A door near the front of the chapel opened, and his thoughts about the case evaporated as Steve Parker's relatives somberly filed in. When he saw Celeste, her sorrowful expression tugged at his heart.

Hank was on one side of her, an older woman he knew had to be her aunt on the other. Fleetingly, he wished once more that he could be right there with her. Then he slowly glanced around the chapel again, searching for anything that didn't seem quite right.

He saw nothing but people who were apparently exactly where they belonged. Come to pay their final respects to Dr. Steve Parker.

As the minister began to speak, Travis's gaze returned to Celeste. Against the black fabric of her dress, her hair and skin seemed even more pale than usual. And she looked utterly vulnerable.

Uneasily, he forced his eyes from her and checked out the others in the chapel one more time. Because she *was* utterly vulnerable. And there was no way in the world he could let anything happen to her.

He loved her. And if he couldn't keep the woman he loved from harm, what kind of man was he?

CHAPTER THIRTEEN

Saturday, October 9, 11:53 a.m.

THERE WAS A RECEPTION upstairs following the service.

At Hank's insistence, Celeste didn't circulate. She simply stood in one corner with him, back to the wall, accepting condolences from those who sought her out. And all the while, she did her best to keep her eyes off Travis.

Only Hank and Evan Reese were aware she knew him. Ideally, no one else should pick up on the fact. Yet as hard as she was trying not to, she found herself constantly checking to see where he was.

"He wouldn't have the nerve," Hank muttered. "Not after yesterday."

When she glanced in the direction he was looking, she saw that Reese had started across the room toward her. Then he hesitated—before finally turning away and saying something to a man standing nearby.

"You were right. He *didn't* have the nerve," she murmured. But she'd bet he would have if Hank hadn't been right beside her, glaring at him.

She eyed Reese for long enough to convince herself he really was going to leave her alone. The next thing she knew, she was gazing at Travis once more. She could tell he was surreptitiously watching her. And watching everyone who came near her.

As emotionally wrung out as she was, his concern still made her feel good—or as close to good as was possible at the moment. He was doing everything he could to help her out of this potential disaster she was in, and—

"Celeste."

She hadn't noticed Bryce approaching, and the sound of his voice made her jump.

"And Detective Ballantyne," he added to Hank.

Normally, Bryce excelled at concealing his thoughts. But not right now. He was clearly wondering what Hank was doing here with her in the first place, let alone sticking to her like a burr to a dog.

"Are you okay?" he asked her.

"All things considered."

After giving her a sympathetic nod, he said, "I'd like to speak to you for a minute."

He glanced pointedly at Hank—who completely ignored the implied message.

"Alone?" he elaborated, giving Hank a longer look.

Celeste nervously licked her lips. She didn't want to talk to him, yet she had a feeling she'd better. Maybe he'd say something that...

She really had no idea what he might say. But listening had to be a smart idea.

"Excuse us for a minute?" she said to Hank.

He didn't seem happy, but he moved off a few feet.

"Why is he with you?" Bryce demanded.

"It's a long story. And it's not what you wanted to talk about."

"No. But...you aren't involved with him, are you?"

She shook her head.

"Then...Celeste...you know, I've been awfully worried about you. All the stress you've been under. First our breakup. Then your mother. Now Steve. I can't help thinking..."

"Thinking what?"

"That you shouldn't have to go through this alone," he said quietly. "And that I miss you."

His words took her aback for a moment. Then she could feel anger starting to build.

"Are you trying to say you've been lonely since Donna left?" she asked, not even attempting to hide her sarcasm.

"She didn't *leave*—I told her to go. And he had no business saying anything about it to you," he added, nodding almost imperceptibly toward Hank.

"He didn't."

"Then who did?"

"That hardly matters, does it."

She could see how badly Bryce wanted a direct answer, and could almost hear him warning himself not to press her.

Finally, he said, "Celeste…"

He paused, raking his fingers through his hair, a clear sign that he didn't feel as in control of the situation as he'd like to.

"I've been doing a lot of thinking," he added at last. "About us."

"Bryce, there *is* no us. There hasn't been for a long time."

"And that's my fault. Entirely. I…being apart from you has made me realize just how badly I screwed up. But…we're still legally married."

She let that pass and simply waited. Obvious as it seemed, she couldn't quite believe where he was heading.

"I know this isn't the time or place," he continued. "But we've got to sit down somewhere, just the two of us, and have a long talk."

Just the two of them? She shivered inside. Was his idea to get her alone so the Ice Man...

"We really don't have anything to talk about," she managed to say evenly. "Unless you mean a divorce, and I'd prefer to have my lawyer handle that discussion."

He shook his head. "I don't want a divorce. I want us to give our marriage another try."

CELESTE HUGGED her cousins and Aunt Nancy goodbye, then started down the stairs with Hank.

"What about Travis?" she asked, glancing back toward the reception room. He was still in there, one of the few remaining people.

"He's watching to see if anyone heads after us. We'll hook up with him later."

As they reached the bottom of the stairs, Hank took her arm and steered her to a rear exit. Outside, a cargo van was waiting.

The driver nodded to them and started the

engine. They climbed into the back and an instant later were on their way.

The van was comfortable enough, with bench seats along the sides, but the interior of the cargo section was dim. The only window was a small one in the door—which Hank immediately commandeered.

He sat wordlessly staring out of it for a few minutes, then said, "I think we're okay. No sign of anyone following us."

"So we're going to Travis's apartment?"

"Not directly. We're taking a little detour to be safe."

He leaned back on the bench and glanced across at her. "I couldn't ask you in there, but my curiosity was killing me. What did Bryce want?"

"I'm not sure. He *said* he wanted to give our marriage another try."

"Really."

She nodded. "He also suggested we get together, *just the two of us,* to discuss it."

"And you told him?"

"Not much. I was afraid of saying the wrong thing, so I told him I was going back to my friend's in Connecticut, and I'd call him in a day or two. We left it at that."

"Did he ask you for your friend's name and number?"

"Yes, but I said it would be better if I called him."

"Good."

She waited, hoping Hank would tell her what he was thinking.

When he didn't, she asked, "Do you figure he's trying to set me up for the Ice Man? That the plan's to convince me to meet him somewhere, and when I get there..." She stopped speaking, her throat suddenly so tight she couldn't go on.

Hank said, "Celeste, keep in mind that we've got a major advantage."

"Which is?"

"We know about the contract. And neither the Ice Man nor Bryce—or *whoever's* behind it—knows we do."

"Ah." She considered that, unable to figure out why knowing a hit man had been paid to kill her was a major advantage.

If Hank believed it was, though, she had to be missing something. Unless he only thought he could make her feel better.

She almost asked if that was it, but decided not to. If they *didn't* actually have an advantage, she'd just as soon delude herself.

Trying to force every thought of the hit man from her mind, she said, "Travis told me you have a little boy."

"Yeah, Robbie. He's almost three this month." He dug out his wallet and showed her a picture.

"Oh, Hank, he's gorgeous. And he looks like you, doesn't he. Has your dark hair and eyes."

"Well...actually, he's adopted."

"Oh?" The instant the word slipped out, she hoped he wouldn't think she was prying.

"My wife...my ex-wife...couldn't have children. And she decided that was what was missing from our marriage. So...well, when Robbie was only a few months old, his parents were killed in an earthquake. In Guatemala. A lot of the children who were orphaned by it were adopted in the U.S., and Robbie ended up with us.

"But instead of making Jane happy, having him only made things worse for her."

Hank gazed at the picture for a moment, then put his wallet back in his pocket and shrugged. "It's ironic, isn't it? She was the one who pressed for the adoption, but I'm the one who ended up being crazy about Robbie. He's just the greatest kid."

Celeste smiled. She had a feeling that even with his awful hours, Hank was a first-rate father.

"We're here," he said.

Through the little window, she could see that they were entering a parking garage.

"This is Manhattan North's garage," he explained. "If anyone is following us, they'll assume I brought you to the precinct to talk about your brother—and wait on the street so they won't miss you leaving. But Travis left his car in here and there's a back way out."

The van driver had obviously been told where Travis's Mustang was parked, because he dropped them off right at it. Not five minutes later, Travis arrived, driving a dark blue Dodge that might as well have been wearing a sign reading Unmarked Police Car.

"Everything okay?" he said, climbing out.

"No sign of anyone," Hank told him.

"Nobody paid any attention when you left the reception, either."

"Which has to mean the Ice Man didn't show."

"I wonder why not," Travis said—almost to himself. "He'd have been certain she'd be there. So why *wouldn't* he decide to follow her? See where she's staying?" Celeste could feel anxiety gnawing at her insides. Despite what he'd told her, Travis had really expected the hit man to be there. "It just seemed an obvious move," he added, slowly shaking his head.

"Maybe he hasn't realized she's not in her own apartment," Hank suggested.

"Maybe."

Travis didn't sound convinced, which made Celeste even more anxious. "You don't think he already knows I'm at your place, do you?" she asked.

He merely shook his head again.

"Well, look, I've got to go in and play catch-up for a while," Hank told them. "If there've been any new developments, I'll let you know."

Travis nodded, then focused on Celeste, quietly asking, "How did you make out at the service? You okay?"

"I'm better since *you* arrived."

Smiling, he wrapped his arms around her and pulled her close.

She rested her cheek against his chest, breathing in his scent. She hadn't realized she'd been cold, but she gradually became aware that his body heat was warming her.

"You know," she whispered at last, "just

being with you like this makes me feel… Oh, I can't even think of the word I want."

"You can't? What kind of an editor *are* you?" he teased.

"The kind who's being *extremely* affected by a handsome man."

"Handsome, huh?" He kissed the top of her head.

"Definitely. A ten on the scale." She snuggled even closer, thinking she'd be happy to stay right here in his arms for ever and a day.

But it was only a few moments before he said, "Let's go home."

Home. With him. That sounded like an even better plan.

TRAVIS SHIFTED the Mustang into drive, dying to know what Bryce Wayland had had to say—but telling himself not to start bombarding Celeste with questions before they even got out of the garage.

He'd give her a little breathing space. Count to a hundred, then ask her.

By the time they reached the back exit, he was at twenty-two. After taking a good long look in each direction, he started for Chelsea, keeping one eye on the rearview mirror, even though he seriously doubted anyone would be on his tail.

Just as he was silently saying "ninety-seven," his cell phone rang. He dug it out of his pocket and answered.

"It's me," Hank said. "Figured you'd like to know that we finally caught up with the low-lifes Steve Parker blew the whistle on. A couple of our fellows questioned them last night."

"And?"

"They've got an alibi. They were in a bar at the time of the murder. Came in around eight and didn't leave until the place shut down."

"Witnesses?"

"Uh-huh. The bartender remembers them because they were complaining about the TV channel he had on."

"And they were both there the whole time?"

"As far as he noticed. He's got some regular customers, and we're in the midst of following up with them. But unless one of them says something different, those two are pretty much in the clear."

"Doesn't leave us with many suspects, does it?"

"Uh-uh. There's Celeste's husband, who we know *doesn't* have an alibi, and our mystery woman in the hall—whose identity we're no closer to having than we were when we started."

"What about the lab results?"

Usually, the crime-scene techs came up with at least *something* that helped the investigators. And every now and then, there was a "something" that blew a case wide open.

"Haven't heard a thing," Hank was saying. "But they've got a ton of work, so it could still be a while. How about Wayland, though? I assume Celeste's filled you in on their conversation?"

"Not yet. I was just getting to that."

"Yeah, well, give me a call later and let me know what you think. Because I'm trying to decide whether it's time to bring him in for questioning."

"Have you turned up *anything* on him?"

"Nothing that helps. As far as we can determine, he's not at all desperate for money. Earns a good buck at his law firm. No major legitimate debts, and no sign that he's a gambler or into drugs. And he's not licensed to own a firearm."

"Well, we both know how easily he could have gotten a gun on the street. And how carefully he'd have disposed of it if he *did* kill Parker."

"Yeah, you're right. But the bottom line is we've still got nothing solid. So I've been thinking I shouldn't tip my hand too soon. That as long as he doesn't realize he's a suspect I should sit tight until I get those lab results. Just keep hoping something in them points at him."

Right, Travis thought. Regardless of how convinced they were of Bryce's guilt, they needed hard evidence.

When it came to building a case, the facts that he had a possible motive and was home alone the night of the murder only added up to a starting point.

"Oh, something else," Hank said. "There's still no sign of Donna Rainfield, and her mother's filed a missing person's. So I've got the option of paying Wayland another visit about her disappearance. Without even mentioning Parker."

"Just off the top, that sounds like the best idea."

"Yeah, well, as I said, let me know what you think after you've talked to Celeste."

"Right. I'll get back to you."

"That was Hank," she said as he tucked the phone away.

"Uh-huh."

"And he said…?"

Briefly, Travis told her. "So he wants to know what I think about your conversation with Bryce," he concluded.

She nodded, then began to recount it.

When she got to the part where Bryce said he wanted to give their marriage another try, Travis's heart froze.

What if she went along with that? What if, regardless of everything, she didn't really believe he was behind the contract? What if she still loved him? More than she loved a man she'd known for almost no time at all?

He exhaled slowly, telling himself that line of thinking was so irrational he must be having some kind of brain seizure.

She'd left Bryce almost a year ago. She'd said they hadn't had much of a marriage even before she'd learned he'd been cheating on her. And she was far too intelligent to be taken in by anything he tried at this late date.

"What's wrong?" she said.

"Nothing. I just can't believe he has that much gall."

"Well, he does. He wants us to get together and discuss how we could work things out. And I'm wondering…I asked Hank this, but he didn't really give me an answer. Do you think Bryce would try to set me up for the Ice Man?"

"It's possible. Or could be he's had second thoughts about killing you. If he wants to lay his hands on your mother's estate, and you went along with the idea of—"

"I wouldn't get back together with him in a million years," she murmured.

Absurd as he realized it was, her words made Travis feel immensely better.

"But you know what I've been thinking?" she continued.

"What?"

"That maybe I *should* agree to meet him for that talk."

He glanced at her, assuming she was joking. But her expression was deadly serious.

"Are you out of your mind?" he said quietly.

"No, listen for a minute. If his idea *is* to set me up, you could turn it from a setup into a trap."

"With you as decoy? Not a chance."

"But I could wear a bulletproof vest. The loose way my coat's cut, if I kept it on the vest wouldn't show. And you could have a dozen cops there, and—"

"And you'd be scared half to death."

"I'm scared half to death, anyway! Travis, I've been living in fear since the minute you told me about the contract. I can't stop thinking about it while I'm awake, and when I fall asleep I have nightmares.

"There's a faceless man with an enormous gun," she continued, "who keeps saying my time is running out and... I just want this to be over. So badly that—"

"No. It's absolutely out of the question. Aside from anything else, it's against department policy to use civilians as decoys."

"Oh? Well I'd rather be a decoy than a sitting duck. Because sooner or later, if you don't get him he's going to get me."

"I'll get him."

"Travis...I know how hard you're trying. But what if he finds me before you find him? Finds me sometime when you're not around? When I'm not wearing a vest and there aren't any cops watching out for me?

"I mean, you're right. I'd be scared. I'd be downright terrified. But at least I'd be doing something that might help bring this to an end."

He didn't reply, just wondered whether he'd be reacting quite so negatively if someone else was offering to play decoy. If it wasn't the woman he loved.

HE'D PRACTICALLY FROZEN his butt off before the black Mustang appeared.

The cop drove by slowly, providing him with a good look into the car. The Langley woman was in the passenger seat.

He took a drag on his cigarette and waited.

They found an empty parking space down the block, and a minute later the two of them were walking toward Quinn's building. He was carrying takeout, which probably meant they weren't just going in to pick up her things.

The Ice Man had figured she might move back to her own apartment after the funeral. Thought she might have only been staying with Quinn until after it was over. That she'd been feeling down and didn't want to be on her own. But now he was thinking she'd be here at least a little longer.

Having established that he still knew exactly where to find her when the time came, he turned and started away—trying to ignore the sense of impatience that had been growing inside him for days now.

In the beginning, this hit had seemed perfectly straightforward. Oh, he didn't usually get told he couldn't pick and choose his own time. Didn't usually have to wait for a go-ahead call.

Still, it wasn't unheard of. Sometimes, a client wanted to be sure that the hit went down when he had an airtight alibi. Like, he was out of the country or something. So the condition hadn't struck him as any big deal at first.

But that was before he'd known how long the call would take in coming. Before he'd known Langley wouldn't stay put in her own place. That he'd have to keep an eye on what she was up to for all this time.

He should be able to charge extra for that. And for her having a boyfriend who was a homicide detective, too.

"I THINK IT'S a good idea," Hank said.

Even before they'd phoned him, Travis had been almost sure that would be his partner's reaction. But he'd been hoping against hope it wouldn't.

He switched his cell to his other ear and glanced at Celeste—sitting on the couch with the cordless.

She shot him a glance that didn't exactly say "I told you, so," but came close.

It made him wish that he'd never introduced her to the conference-call routine. Because if he'd had his way she sure wouldn't be listening in on *this* conversation. Yet when she'd insisted, there hadn't been much he could do to stop her.

He'd learned that if she wanted something badly enough, she got extremely stubborn.

"I don't mean that if Bryce suggests a secluded place you should agree," Hank was saying. "But if he's thinking about a restaurant or something, then I'd say he's *not* trying to set you up. That it's the other alternative. He's decided he'd be smarter to get back together with you, at least for a while, than have you killed. That way, he can still get his hands on the estate, and—"

"Why would he change his mind?" Celeste interrupted.

"Well, maybe whatever actually happened with Donna Rainfield's unnerved him. Or maybe he realized that three deaths by unnatural causes, in the same family, would make us just too suspicious."

"Look, if he's changed his mind, then there's no *point* to them meeting," Travis said.

"Because Celeste getting back together with him is out of the question."

"Yeah, but that doesn't mean a meeting wouldn't be useful. If she can get him talking about her brother, or Donna, she might learn something that'll help us.

"But I think we've got to go with a vest instead of a wire, this time. Just in case I'm guessing wrong. So we have to figure out how you can get away with wearing one, Celeste."

"I've already thought of that. It won't show if I keep my coat on."

"Wait a minute," Travis said. "You two are talking details—as if we've already decided this is the plan. And, Hank, you know Espizito would have our hides if we used a civilian as a decoy."

"Uh-uh. Not under these circumstances. Let's say Celeste told us she was going to meet with Bryce whether we liked it or not. We could hardly *order* her not to. So ensuring her safety would be our obvious move."

"Well, I just don't like the idea," Travis muttered. "I don't like anything about it."

"I know. But just because you don't like it…"

As Hank's words trailed off, Celeste glanced

uneasily at Travis—then said into the phone, "I told Bryce I'd get back to him in a day or so."

"Yeah, you mentioned that."

"But I could do it earlier. I could call him as soon as we're finished talking. Tell him I've been thinking about what he said and…"

"The sooner the better. All I need is time to get things organized, so if you want to set something up for tomorrow—"

"Will you hold on here," Travis snapped, glaring across the room at Celeste. "We still haven't agreed this is the way to go."

"Then let's vote on it," Hank suggested. "I vote she does it."

Travis continued to look at Celeste, willing her to rethink the idea.

She held his gaze for a long moment, then said, "I vote with Hank."

CHAPTER FOURTEEN

Saturday, October 9, 4:18 p.m.

WHEN BRYCE ANSWERED his phone, Celeste took a deep breath, then said, "Hi, it's me."

She glanced at Travis as she spoke.

He was sitting on the far end of the couch, listening in on his cell. And although she knew he was still unhappy about her doing this, he gave her an encouraging thumbs-up.

"Well, hello," Bryce was saying. "I didn't expect to hear from you so soon."

She uneasily licked her lips. He sounded as pleased that she'd called him as he used to way back when. But they were light-years beyond those days.

"Yes, well, I changed my mind about Connecticut. Decided I'd wait a day or two before heading up there again. And I've been considering what you said."

"Good. Then how about dinner tonight?"

Dinner. A restaurant, not a secluded place.

That sounded as if Hank had guessed right. But he needed more than a couple of hours' lead time.

Feeling a bit less nervous, she said, "I'm afraid tonight won't work. What about tomorrow, though? Maybe just meet somewhere for coffee?"

"Why don't we compromise. Do lunch."

She'd known he'd never let her off with just coffee, so they were a step ahead of him on that. Before she'd called, they'd checked that Zia's was open for both lunch and dinner on Sundays. The surveillance had been so easy when she'd met Evan Reese there, it only made sense to use the restaurant again.

"Lunch," she said slowly. "Well…sure, that would be nice. Do you want to try a new place I discovered?"

"Anywhere you'd like."

She'd anticipated that response, too. Bryce was always easy to get along with when he wanted something.

"It's called Zia's," she told him. "Just down the block from Joe Allen. Why don't I meet you there around one."

"I'll come by your place. Pick you up. A little after twelve-thirty?"

"No, I'll be out in the morning. I've got

a few things to do. So meeting you makes more sense."

"Oh, okay. But I'll drive you home afterward. Maybe come in and pay Snoops a visit."

She glanced at Travis again.

He shook his head, even though he had to know there wasn't the slightest doubt in her mind. There was no way she intended to be all alone with her ex-husband.

"How's he doing?" Bryce asked.

For a second she didn't realize he meant Snoops—the cat he'd basically ignored when they'd lived together.

"Fine," she said. "He's fine."

"Good. Well...tomorrow then. I'll make reservations."

"Yes, we might need them. It's not a very big place."

"Then I'll call now. And Celeste?"

"Uh-huh?"

"I'm really happy you got in touch right away."

"Oh, no," she murmured as he clicked off. "He figures I'm *eager* to get together with him."

"Don't worry about it," Travis told her. "I'll phone Hank. Let him know we're on. And it's supposed to be cold again tomorrow. So if he tells the owner to give you that table by the door, you'll have a perfect excuse to keep your coat on."

She nodded, trying not to think about the reason she'd be wearing a Kevlar vest under it.

"But I'll have to be there first," she said. "Because if they try to give Bryce that table he'll insist on a better one."

"We'll get you there in plenty of time."

As Travis pressed the speed dial for Hank's number, Snoops came skulking into the room and leaped onto the couch between them. Celeste absently stroked the cat while she listened to Travis's side of the conversation.

After it was over, he said, "Hank was thinking about paying Bryce another visit in the morning, but now he's going to leave it until after your lunch. See how that goes first."

She nodded, then waited, expecting him to say something more. When he merely sat gazing at her, she said, "What are you thinking?"

Travis shrugged. He didn't want to tell her the truth—that he'd been thinking how much he loved her. And about how, if Bryce *was* setting her up...

"Travis? You're still upset that Hank and I outvoted you, aren't you."

"Yeah, I am. I'd far rather you'd just stay far away from Bryce. But that wasn't what I was thinking."

"No? Then…"

He mentally scrambled for something and decided on, "I was thinking that once this is over you'll have to meet my family."

She smiled a smile that made him love her even more. Which was pretty unbelievable, considering he wouldn't have imagined "more" was possible.

"I'd like that," she said softly.

"And they'll like you."

"I hope so."

Her words made his pulse race.

Oh, he hadn't forgotten what she'd said mere days ago. That they should wait until this situation was resolved. See how they felt about each other at that point.

And even though the "waiting" had pretty much gone by the boards, he knew that didn't necessarily mean she was contemplating a future together—something he just couldn't stop himself from doing.

But if she cared about whether his family liked her…

He told himself it was a promising sign. That was *all* it was, though.

"I wish we could go out," she said quietly. "Just for a walk or something. I enjoy walking."

Suddenly, he was imagining long walks with her. Wandering around the South Street Seaport. Heading up to the top of Manhattan to explore the Cloisters. Window shopping on Fifth Avenue. And Central Park was only a couple of blocks from her apartment.

There was so much to see in the city that they could walk forever if she liked. But not until this was over.

The odds that the wrong person would see them, would figure out that she was staying here, had to be eight million to one. But he didn't want to take even that slight a chance.

"Now you've got me wanting to go out, too," he said. "It's not a good idea, though."

"I know. It's just that I've only been out twice since I got here. Yesterday, to meet Evan Reese. Then today, to Steve's…" She shook her head. "I still feel so badly about him, Travis."

He slid closer to her—prompting Snoops to leap off the couch. When her gaze met his, her eyes were as blue as the sea and glistening with tears.

"Oh, Celeste," he murmured, wrapping his arms around her.

She buried her face against his shoulder and hugged him hard. He thought she was crying but wasn't sure. Then he felt her tears on his neck.

"Things are going to get better," he said into her hair. "I promise."

"And do you always keep your promises?" she whispered.

"Yes. Always."

After a long minute of silence, she eased away far enough that she could look at him and said, "Travis, if I didn't have you I don't know what I'd do."

He smiled, aware his heartbeat was accelerating. "Then it's a good thing you've got me, isn't it?"

She did her best to smile back. "It's a *very* good thing," she murmured before she leaned closer again and kissed him.

That was all it took. He was instantly lost in her warmth, her softness, her sultry scent. Lost in his love for her.

TRAVIS LOCKED HIS apartment door, then led the way downstairs, ordering himself to act cool. Anything else would only make Celeste more nervous.

When they reached the front door, he gave her a lingering kiss before opening it. Then he checked the street to be sure there was no one just standing around, keeping an eye on his place.

There wasn't. Of course, that didn't mean someone wasn't watching from one of the parked cars—using the angles to prevent being seen.

Reminding himself the Ice Man had no way of knowing Celeste was here, he took her hand and started down the outside steps.

Just as predicted, it was another chilly day. Even so, while he walked her to the yellow cab waiting at the curb he could feel himself sweating.

Once she was in the back seat, he headed around to the driver's open window and asked the undercover officer playing cabbie to take good care of her.

"You've got it," the man said.

"See you later," he told Celeste through the window.

The tight smile she gave him made him wish he could have ridden along with her. But they just couldn't risk that.

He remained where he was until the taxi disappeared from sight, making sure that none of those parked cars pulled out and followed it. Then he strode down the block to his Mustang.

Barely fifteen minutes later, he was walking into the restaurant directly across the street from Zia's.

As promised, a table had been reserved for him at the front window. It afforded a perfect view of Celeste, already there waiting.

He ordered the lunch special, even though he knew he was too anxious to eat, and settled in to watch—trying, one more time, to convince himself that this would be a complete nonevent.

Celeste probably wasn't in any danger at all. Not when Wayland had most likely changed his mind about the contract. In fact, he might have already called it off.

Well, no, that was being overly optimistic. He'd wait until he saw how things went with her. But even if they went badly, from his perspective, the Ice Man *wouldn't* try to make his hit in a restaurant.

However, just on the off chance he might, Hank had taken every possible precaution.

The alley door was locked and a uniform

was back there again. No one would be able to sneak in unnoticed.

Also like last time, detectives were both inside Zia's and on the street. Plus, Celeste was wearing the vest.

He couldn't help wishing she had on a wire, as well, but the vest would smother the sounds of any normal-level conversation. Besides, it didn't really matter that he couldn't listen in, because nothing was going to go wrong.

Unless, of course, the Ice Man *did* make his move—and shot her in the head.

Travis told himself that couldn't conceivably happen. Hank's people would be on him long before he could get off a shot.

At least, that was how the scene was supposed to play out. *If* the hit man showed. Which he *shouldn't*.

"Travis?"

He looked up to find Hank standing beside him, his expression strained.

"What's wrong?" he demanded, instantly assuming Celeste was in a lot more danger than he'd been telling himself.

But what Hank said as he sat down was "My father's had a heart attack and it's touch-and-go."

"Oh…man…I'm sorry," he said quietly. He knew Hank was close to his parents.

"It was my uncle who called. My mother's in such bad shape she can't even talk on the phone. I've got to get to Chicago."

"As soon as you can."

Hank nodded. "I'm already booked. The plane leaves in two hours, so I've pretty well got to head for the airport right now."

"What about Robbie?" Taking off on short notice had to be hard when you had a child to worry about.

"Mrs. Chevalier said they'll be fine."

"Thankfully you have a great housekeeper, huh?"

"Exactly. But, look, I'm sorry I've got to leave with everything the way it—"

"Don't even think about it. I just hope your father comes through all right. And call me after you get there, okay? Let me know how he's doing?"

Hank nodded again. "And I'll phone Koscina on my way to the airport. He's already figured out that you're unofficially still involved with the case. So I'll tell him that if there's anything you need to know he should fill you in on the quiet."

"Thanks."

Koscina, the detective who'd replaced Travis as the other primary on the Parker case, was an all-right guy. So if Travis *did* need anything it shouldn't be a problem.

But he'd feel a whole lot better if Hank wasn't going to Chicago.

CELESTE SPOTTED BRYCE before he saw her— walking down the street, watching for the address.

Despite the cold, he wasn't wearing a coat. Just a perfectly tailored three-piece suit that looked new and a silk tie that looked expensive. Dressed to kill.

When the phrase formed in her mind, her pulse began to race and her throat felt dry.

Even though she was almost certain he wouldn't, personally, try to harm her, and even though Travis kept assuring her that hit men didn't like places where there'd be witnesses…

As Bryce breezed into the restaurant, she told herself not to let him know how frightened she felt. But she wasn't the actress. Donna was.

Donna, who had disappeared without a trace.

That thought made it tough to return the warm smile Bryce gave her.

"I'm not late, am I?" he said, glancing at his Rolex.

"No, I was early."

He smiled again, and kissed her cheek. She managed not to cringe.

"Aren't you taking off your coat?"

"Maybe in a bit. Right now, I'm a little chilly."

"Then why don't we get another table. Away from the door."

"No, this one's fine. I like sitting near the windows. Watching the world go by."

"Uh-huh, you always did."

The waiter was at their table before they could say anything more, and Bryce ordered a bottle of Orvieto without either asking if that was all right with her or looking at the wine list.

"So," he said as the man turned away. "This friend in Connecticut. You met her recently?"

As in, he meant, since he didn't know her, it must have been after they'd broken up.

"Yes. She's a freelance editor, too, and we worked on a series together. For Harper," she added, thinking that detailed lies were probably more convincing.

Bryce nodded as if he were sincerely interested in her work, although he never had been when they were together.

The waiter arrived back with the wine and they silently sat through the uncorking-and-tasting ritual.

Once he was gone again, Bryce held his glass up in a toast. "To us."

She forced her glass to her lips, but couldn't make herself take a sip. She had an almost overwhelming urge to simply repeat what she'd told him yesterday, to say there *was* no us. But the plan involved getting him talking, not making him angry.

"You said you've been thinking about what I suggested," he continued.

"Yes, I have."

"We had a lot of good times together, Celeste."

"We did," she agreed, although "a lot" was a decided exaggeration.

"And I've learned my lesson. I really have."

"Well, I guess that's one of my biggest problems with your proposition," she said slowly.

"The way I moved out and Donna moved right in made me realize you didn't really care that I'd left. And if you'd reached the stage of having so little feeling for me, I don't see how—"

"Celeste, that wasn't it. I hadn't stopped loving you—I just made a stupid mistake. I know that now. I realized it almost immediately. But she gave me an ultimatum. Said that either she moved in with me or we were through. And I was so upset because *you* were gone...

"There's no point in dwelling on that, though. As I said, I made a mistake—both by getting involved with Donna in the first place and by giving in to what she wanted. And I know I can't apologize enough for being such an idiot. But she's completely out of the picture now."

"You're sure about that? She's turned up and you've talked to her?"

"Well...no, I haven't heard from her. And I can't say that makes me unhappy. Celeste, she's a crazy woman. So crazy I can't believe I didn't realize that when I first met her.

"But the important thing is she's out of my life now. And I don't want her back in it. I want *you* back."

When he covered her hand with his, she resisted the urge to pull hers away.

"No matter what Donna might say or do in the future," he continued, "I—"

"Small world, isn't it."

Celeste's startled glance flashed to Evan Reese. He'd materialized beside their table and was staring at Bryce's hand on hers.

"You here again, me here again," he said, his gaze shifting to her face. "Must be a function of our cosmic connection."

She simply removed her hand from Bryce's and said nothing, but she knew it was far more likely a function of her having told him she came here all the time.

Out of the corner of her eye, she could see a couple at a nearby table looking her way— and realized they must be the detectives Hank had promised.

All right, then. She could relax. If things got out of hand, they'd step in. But surely she could deal with Evan Reese. She'd had enough practice over the past little while.

When she turned toward him once more, he smiled as if they were best buddies. Then he glanced curiously at Bryce and she had to introduce them.

"I saw you yesterday," Reese said as Bryce rose to shake hands. "After the service. You seemed to be having such an intense conversation with Celeste that I wondered who you were."

"I'm her husband," Bryce told him, sitting down again.

Reese's expression went cold. Celeste stopped breathing. She didn't know what he'd say next, but she was certain it wouldn't make her happy.

"Your husband," he said slowly, staring at her. "I thought you were divorced."

"You thought wrong," Bryce said, smiling to show he was merely clearing up the misconception—in a friendly way.

Reese icily said, "Really," and didn't smile back.

Bryce caught her gaze and silently asked her to explain what was going on.

She only wished she knew. Reese was the proverbial loose cannon.

"Well, you *are* a busy woman, aren't you," Reese said. "I'm starting to wonder if there's room for me in your life. I mean, between a husband and a boyfriend…"

She didn't say a word when he paused, and she knew Bryce wasn't about to, either. As curious as he had to be, he was too smart to let Reese manipulate him into any sort of scene.

Finally, Reese turned to him and said, "You *do* know about the boyfriend, don't you? The police detective?"

"Of course," he said smoothly. "Detective Ballantyne. You probably saw me talking to *him* after the service, too."

"Detective *Ballantyne?*" Reese's voice jumped an octave on Hank's name.

"You're even busier than I thought," he told Celeste.

Then he looked at Bryce again. "No, I meant Detective Travis Quinn. *He's* the one she's practically living with. Or maybe I should leave out the *practically.*"

CHAPTER FIFTEEN

Sunday, October 10, 1:41 p.m.

CELESTE STOPPED BREATHING once more. How did Reese know she was staying with Travis? Should she ask him or not? And if he knew, who else did?

Both he and Bryce were staring at her now, and she simply couldn't decide what to do.

"You're wondering how I found out what you and Quinn are up to, aren't you," Reese said at last.

She gave him the most casual shrug she could manage.

"Well, I wanted to talk to you Friday night. I felt uncomfortable about the way we'd left things between us. We were here for lunch," he explained to Bryce. "And we had a bit of a...disagreement.

"At any rate," he said, turning back to Celeste, "I figured if I phoned I'd only get your machine, so I decided to pay you a visit. And when you weren't home, I waited. Only, you never showed."

"Are you saying you waited all night?" Bryce asked.

"My car has a good heater. It was comfortable enough. But the whole time," he continued to Celeste, "I was wondering where you could be. Then yesterday, at the service, I realized where.

"Quinn was there, pretending he wasn't paying the slightest attention to you but actually keeping an eye on you the whole time.

"I found that pretty strange, until I figured out that the two of you just didn't want people to realize you were…close. Then it struck me that maybe you'd gotten *really* close.

"So this morning, when you weren't home again, I went down to West Twenty-eighth—his address is in the book. And after I sat watching from my car for a while, what do you think I saw? You and him coming out of his place, acting all lovey-dovey before you got into that cab."

Reese had clearly finished his explanation, but Celeste just didn't know what she should say.

There was a long moment of silence, then Bryce said, "Well, it sounds as if you should be a detective yourself, Mr. Reese. And it was nice meeting you. But before you arrived, Celeste and I were in the middle of discussing something important, so…"

"So you'd like me to leave."

When neither she nor Bryce corrected his conclusion, Reese said, "Well. Enjoy your lunch."

Without even looking at her again, he turned away.

As he walked out of the restaurant, she murmured, "Thank you," to Bryce.

"You handled that really well," she added— thinking that right this instant she was feeling far more kindly toward him than she had in a long time.

Then she remembered the contract and went cold inside.

"Who *is* he?" Bryce said, his voice quiet, but his tone telling her he was angry.

"He was a patient of Steve's. And for some reason he's convinced that we should be friends."

"I see. And what about this Detective Travis Quinn?"

She tried merely shrugging, although she knew it would only buy her a few seconds.

"*Are* you living with him?"

"No. Not exactly."

"What does that mean?"

"It's a long story."

"I've got all afternoon."

He waited, glaring at her, while she racked her brain for something to say.

She didn't intend to tell him she was staying with Travis because of the contract on her. Not after Hank had said that knowing about it when the Ice Man wasn't aware they knew was a big advantage.

Finally, Bryce drained his wineglass, then said, "Well, I hope you enjoyed your revenge—even if it did get cut short."

"My revenge?"

"How long were you going to keep it up? Pretending you were actually considering a reconciliation with me, when you're living with some cop?"

She nervously licked her lips, thinking that keeping quiet had to be her best move.

"You know, I'm starting to wonder if I've got a serious problem when it comes to women," he muttered. "I totally misread Donna. And I lived with you for three years without realizing you'd ever do anything as calculatedly cruel as this. So, as I said, I hope you enjoyed it."

With that, Bryce rose, tossed a couple of twenties onto the table, then strode out to the street.

TRAVIS WAS STILL SITTING in the restaurant across from Zia's, his breathing pretty well back to normal.

His body had gone onto red alert when Evan Reese had shown up. And it had stayed that way while he'd watched the pantomime that ensued between Celeste, Reese and Wayland.

The entire time, he'd been wishing he could hear as well as see. But at least he knew that nothing awful had happened. And he'd managed to more or less relax once Reese left.

Now, with Wayland marching angrily down the sidewalk, both men were gone.

After paying his bill, he gazed over at Celeste again. He wanted to be with her right this second, but he'd be smarter to stay where he was for a few more minutes, in case Reese or Wayland reappeared.

Finally, he pushed back his chair and started for the door. Outside, there was no sign of either man—although that didn't guarantee they were both really gone.

Celeste spotted him when he was halfway across the street, and her relief was apparent. It made him wonder if there'd *ever* come a time when she'd simply look glad to see him, when she wouldn't be living in fear.

Several people in Zia's glanced at him as he walked in. Two of them, a couple sitting near Celeste, he made as detectives.

He gave them a subtle nod, thinking they'd probably overheard at least some of what had been said, which put them ahead of him.

"Am I glad to see *you*," Celeste murmured as he reached her.

He was dying to wrap his arms around her and hug her half to death. Instead, he merely said, "After the company you've been keeping, I'm not surprised. But come on, let's get out of here."

He led the way to the back door and into the alley, speaking briefly to the uniform posted there, then taking Celeste's hand and starting rapidly in the direction of his car.

"So what happened?" he asked as they walked.

By the time they reached the Mustang, she'd finished telling him.

Before he started the engine, he gave her

that hug, and holding her felt so good it required a major effort to stop. But he wanted to get away from here.

"Where are we going?" she asked as he pulled out of the parking garage.

Good question. His apartment was obviously no longer an option. Now that Wayland knew where she'd been staying, the Ice Man would, as well. So where *did* they go?

After considering and rejecting a few possibilities, he settled on one he liked. That decision made, he figured he'd better tell her about Hank's father.

"Oh, Travis," she murmured after he had. "Hank must be feeling…"

He glanced at her and she shook her head. "I know exactly how he's feeling. My father died of a sudden heart attack. Then my mother…well, I'm only too aware of how losing a parent hits people.

"You never really think about what an important part of your life your parents are, a part that's always been there. Then, suddenly, poof, there's a big void. And you wouldn't believe how often you find yourself thinking about him. Or her."

He reached for her hand, trying to imagine how it would be to walk into his parents' place and not have his mother hurry to hug him. Or his father make some corny remark about hoping he'd try to not eat them out of house and home this time.

"What about his little boy?" Celeste asked.

"He'll be okay. Their housekeeper is like a grandmother to him."

Turning his attention back to his driving, he cut over to Ninth, where the traffic was lighter. After that, it didn't take long to reach the unpretentious little Shantyre Hotel.

When they got there he parked in the lot beside it, choosing a space at the rear and snugging the Mustang up close to the car facing it so his plates couldn't be seen without effort.

For half a second, he debated asking Celeste to wait in the car while he made sure Al Catucci was still the manager. But he didn't really want her out of his sight, so he took her inside with him.

"This way," he said, starting across the modest lobby.

He ignored the desk clerk, who looked as though he couldn't care less about them, anyway, and headed directly to the manager's office—offering up a silent prayer of thanks when he saw that Al's name was still on the door.

It was half-open, so he just gave a single knock and stuck his head in.

"Detective Quinn," Al said, grinning at him. "Good to see you. What can I do for you?" he added as they stepped inside.

"We need a safe place to lay low for a night or two."

Al didn't say another word. He simply rose from his desk and walked out of the office. A minute later he was back with a room key.

"Stay for as long as you need to," he said, handing it over. "And nobody will know who you are except me."

"Thanks. I appreciate this a lot."

"No problem. October's a low-occupancy month."

Celeste murmured a thank-you. Then, once they'd started for the room, quietly said, "A good friend?"

"Actually, just an acquaintance. But this place is in the two-four precinct, which is where I worked before I joined Homicide. And my partner and I defused a situation here a few years ago. Something that might have cost Al his job. I was hoping he hadn't forgotten."

They walked the rest of the way in silence, and once they were inside their room Travis reached for Celeste and kissed her.

They had a lot of thinking to do, but it could wait for a while. At the moment, reminding her how much he cared was more important.

"I'LL BE THERE," the Ice Man said into his cellular.

"You're clear on exactly where it is."

"Yeah, I've got it."

"And you understand you have to be right on time. That's crucial."

"Of course I understand," he muttered, his annoyance growing with every stupid instruction.

"Good, then I'll see you."

"Yeah." He clicked off and tossed the phone onto his bed, telling himself not to worry. He'd been waiting so long for the go-ahead call that he should just be glad it had finally come. Problem was, this job kept bothering him more and more.

He didn't mind too much being told when. Not usually. But the "when" had never been this specific before. That really bugged him.

Like he was a kid being reminded to get to school on time or something.

And he didn't like being told where. Didn't like that at all.

He'd scoped out Celeste Langley's street. Then Travis Quinn's. Had figured out how he could get in and out of the areas fast. Possible escape routes if there was any problem.

But now, to walk into a strange place, cold...

Cold. He was the Ice Man, why should he be concerned about walking into a place cold?

His little joke didn't make him smile. Maybe his client figured this was the perfect place for a hit, but his client wasn't the pro.

Still, it sounded all right. Sounded pretty good, actually. No one anywhere around except him, the client and his target. But things weren't always as good as people made them out to be.

Shaking his head, he wished once again that he'd never taken the money for this job. Or that he'd asked for double his regular fee.

Because what he didn't like most of all was surprises. In this case, being hit with a major change at the last moment.

Tomorrow, he decided, he'd pay that little creep Giovanni a visit. And make it real clear he didn't want the guy sending him any more clients with marbles where their brains should be.

Travis had showered first, and when he came out of the bathroom Celeste was sitting on the bed with the pillows propped up against the headboard and the top sheet tucked modestly around her.

She was apparently lost in thought, so he wandered over to the window and just stood gazing out.

After a while, he turned from the window and said, "What are you thinking?"

She gave him a wan smile. "About how I told Evan Reese that Zia's was one of my favorite restaurants. And how I'm glad it really isn't. Because I'll never be able to show my face in there again.

"I mean, twice now, the man I was supposed to have lunch with stormed out on me. Without ordering any food. If they saw me coming again they'd lock the door."

Travis gave her major points for even *trying* to see humor in what had happened, then said, "You know what?"

"What?"

"That's the absolute least of our worries.

There are a zillion restaurants where you'll still be welcome."

"You're right. And having to leave Snoops on his own tonight isn't a serious problem, either. There's lots of food down. He'll be fine."

He nodded, aware they were making small talk to avoid getting into a discussion about where they should go from here.

Maybe that was because they were both feeling as if they didn't have many options, although he *did* have an idea. He was just reluctant to tell her about it because it involved her. And, ideally, she shouldn't leave this room until he'd gotten to the bottom of things.

But considering how little progress he'd made thus far, that might take forever. And he doubted she'd go for the idea of being cooped up indefinitely.

"What would you think about staying here for longer than a night or two?" he asked, deciding to test the waters.

She held his gaze for a moment, then said, "I could live with that. As long as you're here with me."

"Well, I'd be gone some of the time."

"Travis…I don't want to be alone in a strange place. Sitting here, jumping at every sound. We considered my going to a hotel in the first place, remember? Before we decided I'd stay with you. And...I'd just be too nervous."

"Then maybe you should leave town. And I'm not talking about a fictional friend in Connecticut. I'm thinking far away. San Francisco or someplace."

She slowly shook her head. "Go to San Francisco or someplace and worry myself sick about you? Because that's all I'd do."

"Really?"

"You haven't figured that out by now?"

Lowering himself onto the bed beside her, he wrapped his arms around her.

"Travis, I want to be wherever you are," she whispered.

And he wanted to be wherever she was. He wanted to hold her close, just the way he was doing right now, and never let her go.

He loved her so much he could hardly believe it. And if she really felt that same insane way about him...

He just *had* to bring this nightmare to an end. Then they could get on with their lives. Together.

The word began echoing in his head, but he didn't speak it aloud. That would only be tempting fate.

Yet wasn't that exactly what he'd be doing if he involved her in something that could be dangerous? As much as he didn't want to risk that...

Celeste tensed in his arms when his cell began to ring.

"It's okay," he said. "No one has any idea where we are."

He answered the call and Hank said, "Hey, it's me."

His tone was upbeat, so things couldn't be a total disaster in Chicago.

"Glad you called," Travis told him. "How's your father?"

"Well, he's in intensive care. But they've got back some test results and the damage isn't too bad. Nothing like they were afraid it might be."

"That's great, Hank."

He repeated the news to Celeste and she smiled. "Tell him I'm aiming all my positive vibes toward Chicago."

"She says she's positive-vibing you."

"Yeah, well, thank her for me. My mom's doing better, too. Hearing that Dad'll probably pull through made a world of difference."

"I'll bet."

"At any rate, I'll hang in here till we're certain he's on the mend, but I shouldn't be away for too long. So, how are things there?"

"Actually, we've run into a problem."

"I'm going to shower," Celeste whispered.

As she headed for the bathroom, Travis began telling Hank about what had happened at Zia's.

After he was finished, Hank muttered, "You know, you were right. We *should* have charged Reese with something. I don't care who his uncle is. If it had made him back off, it would have been worth a hassle. But what are you going to do now?"

"I'm still considering."

What he'd like to do, right this minute, was discuss his idea with Hank. Get his thoughts on it.

But the shower had stopped running, which meant that Celeste would be back out here any second. And he didn't want her to know what he was thinking until he decided whether he was willing to involve her.

"Well, you take care, buddy," Hank said. "And if you want to talk about what's happening, just call. I've got my phone with me, so I'm just a speed dial away."

"Thanks. I might do that." But he probably wouldn't. With his father lying in an ICU,

Hank didn't need anything more to worry about.

As he put down his phone, the bathroom door opened and Celeste appeared—dressed again, but with her hair still damp.

"That's wonderful news about Hank's dad," she said. "From what you initially told me, I was fearing the worst."

He nodded slowly, buying himself a few seconds of thinking time. If he tried going to talk to Bryce Wayland on his own, would the guy even see him? And if he did…

His best guess was that he wouldn't get very far without Celeste's help. So as uneasy as it made him…

Telling himself he just didn't have a choice, he said, "I want to run something by you."

She nodded.

"I'm thinking we might be able to force things to a head by paying Bryce a visit."

"We," she said slowly. "You mean the two of us."

"I would never let you go see him alone. Not without Hank here to orchestrate backup. So…are you game for another session with him?"

"Of course. Just tell me what we're trying to do."

He picked up his phone again and handed it to her. "First, call and see whether he's home. Just click off if he answers, though."

He'd rather not alert Bryce to the fact that they were coming—in case *he* alerted the Ice Man. But he certainly wasn't going to say that to Celeste.

She pressed in a number, held the phone to her ear for a minute, then clicked off. "He's there."

"Good, then we're on."

"Okay, so we go to his apartment and…"

"Well, we can fine-tune this on our way there. But, basically, you'll say you're so upset about what happened in the restaurant that you just had to talk to him. That you want to tell him what's *really* been going on with the two of us.

"Not that you'll actually do that. You'll say we *aren't* involved with each other and you *were* seriously considering the idea of getting back together with him.

"And that you asked me to come along to help you explain why you've been staying at my place—since it's such an incredible story."

"And the incredible story is…?"

"The truth. Or parts of it, at least. We tell

him that while Hank was asking around about your brother, he learned there was a contract on you. And, naturally, he told you about it so you could take precautions. But, not surprisingly, it made you really upset."

"So upset that I totally freaked out," Celeste said, continuing the thought. "Bryce would certainly believe that. Every time I talk to him he starts going on about all the stress I've been under."

"Good. So you freaked out and Hank was trying to come up with a way of helping you.

"And it occurred to him that since I was just starting a couple of weeks' leave I might agree to hire out as a bodyguard. You think Bryce would believe *that?*"

She shrugged uncertainly. "He *might,* although he'd wonder why I didn't hire a *real* bodyguard. Someone who does it as his full-time job, I mean."

"Because you wanted protection starting right then. And it would have taken a while to arrange…"

Travis paused, reminding himself that Wayland wasn't stupid. He'd be suspicious of everything they told him. Still, they'd be catching him off guard, and if he said just one wrong thing…

"We'll have to play it by ear after we get started," he said at last.

"But the important thing is that we tell him we know about the contract and see how he reacts. Because he'll immediately wonder if we're aware that *he's* behind it."

"Travis?" Celeste said slowly.

"What?"

"How much trouble could you get in for doing this? With the department?"

"I'm not sure. None if nobody hears about it."

"But if somebody does?"

"It might not be a big problem."

"Really?"

He shrugged. "I won't be going to see him as a cop. I'll be going as your friend."

Of course, he actually had no idea whether that would make any difference to the C.O. Right this minute, though, he couldn't care less.

The only thing he cared about was that nothing happened to Celeste.

CHAPTER SIXTEEN

Sunday, October 10, 8:47 p.m.

CELESTE HADN'T BEEN back to the apartment she'd shared with Bryce since the day she'd walked out on him, and the closer they got to Murray Hill the more anxious she felt.

But the prospect of setting foot in the apartment again wasn't what was bothering her. It was thinking about what might happen while they were there.

If Bryce *had* killed Steve, then he had a gun. No, she corrected herself. According to Travis, he'd have gotten rid of it.

He could have bought another one, though, and... Or maybe *nothing* would happen.

Despite the way everything seemed to point to Bryce's guilt, she still wasn't *entirely* convinced he was the villain of the piece, was still having trouble believing she could have lived with him for three years without realizing he was capable of—

"Okay," Travis said, turning onto East Thirty-sixth. "Which one is it?"

"That one ahead on the right." She pointed to the stately old building that dated back to the late-nineteenth century.

"Nice."

She nodded. A lot of Manhattan's once-prestigious neighborhoods had faded from glory, but not Murray Hill. It was the personification of historic charm.

"I'll just find a place to park, and—"

"No. Wait. That's Bryce standing out front. That's his car pulling up."

Travis quickly stopped the Mustang, and they watched while the valet got out of Bryce's silver Porsche and he climbed in. He was dressed casually—for him, at least. Tailored pants, deck shoes and a custom-made buttery leather jacket that she recalled had cost a small fortune.

"There's no sense in just sitting around waiting for him to come home," Travis said as the car pulled away. "We might as well see where he's going."

Bryce drove to Second Avenue and turned south. They followed along, Travis hanging half a block back.

Eventually, they cut over to Broadway and started south again, in Greenwich Village now.

"Any idea where he's going?" Travis said.

"None."

A few blocks farther along, Bryce turned onto Bleeker Street. It was a mix of low-rise tenements, storefronts, cafés and clubs. Some of the buildings were renovated; others looked as if the only things keeping them upright were their next-door neighbors.

"Is he the club type?" Travis asked as the Porsche crawled past a line of people waiting for admission to some obviously trendy spot.

"He didn't used to be."

"Well, he's either looking for an address or a place to park."

A few moments later, Bryce found a space and began maneuvering the Porsche into it.

"Duck down," Travis ordered.

She ducked.

"Okay, we're by him."

When she sat up again they were a hundred yards farther along the street and parking next to a garage-type door with a sign reading:

Deliveries Only
ABSOLUTELY NO PARKING
Offenders Will Be Tagged And Towed
Enforced 24 Hours A Day

"I take it we're ignoring that?" Celeste said.

He shrugged. "We don't have time to look for another spot. Come on," he added, switching off the interior roof light before he opened his door.

By the time she climbed out of the car, Bryce was rapidly walking back the way they'd come. Travis grabbed her hand and they started after him.

When he got to Broadway, he crossed to the other side and headed down a street just north of Bleeker.

It didn't seem to have a street sign. It also didn't have any lights. Or if it did they weren't working.

She couldn't help thinking they'd probably been shot out, and that made her frightened enough to be very glad she knew Travis was wearing his gun.

Up ahead, between two dilapidated hulks of buildings, was an alley—a faint glow filtering from it. The dark shadow that was Bryce disappeared into it.

Celeste and Travis hurried forward, then stopped a few feet from the opening.

Travis pressed her against the old building and told her to wait right there.

Then, reaching under his jacket, he drew his gun and stepped toward the alley.

IT SEEMED TO CELESTE that an eternity passed before Travis eased back toward her, reholstered his gun and stepped away from the building to have a look at it.

"What?" she whispered.

"This is the Winslow Lane Theater," he said. "Ring a bell?"

When nothing came to her, she moved over to where he was standing and gazed at the facade. Sure enough, it was a run-down old theater.

The poster behind the wire mesh on the door advertised a play called *Talking Too Loud,* running from September 4 through October 9.

October 9th. Yesterday. The day of Steve's memorial service. The end of the play's run.

Tonight, the theater was dark and deserted.

She eyed the poster, certain she'd never heard of *Talking Too Loud.* Yet something was tugging at her memory.

Then she recalled that Carol Schoenberg had mentioned the Winslow Lane Theater.

"This is where Donna Rainfield was acting," she said.

"You got it. And guess who just let Bryce in the stage door."

"Donna?"

Travis nodded.

"You're *certain?*"

"Uh-huh. There's a light over the door. It's not too bright, but it was shining directly on her, and she looks exactly like that picture Hank showed us. Besides, who else would Bryce be coming here to see?"

"Right," she murmured.

"She must have had a key while she was in the play and kept it."

"I guess. But what's going on? Why is Bryce here?"

"I haven't got a clue," Travis admitted. "At least now, though, we know he didn't kill her."

Yet.

The word formed in the darkness, like a little neon sign before his eyes. Was *that* why Bryce was here?

Had he come to dispose of the crazy lady who'd trashed his apartment? Who'd then vanished, probably hoping people would wonder if he'd had something to do with her disappearance?

And maybe she'd done more to cause him grief. Things they knew nothing about.

If so, he might well have decided he'd had enough. Especially if he'd murdered Steve Parker and figured he'd gotten away with that. If he could succeed once, why not twice?

Travis uneasily rubbed his jaw. If Bryce was here to kill Donna, he had to prevent it from happening.

"I'd *love* to know what's going on in there," Celeste said.

So would he. Man, would he ever.

He considered the situation.

He'd noticed the door hadn't closed tightly after Donna let Bryce in. The thought that they should be more careful had crossed his mind.

However, since they hadn't been, getting into the theater would be no problem.

But going in and leaving Celeste out here wasn't an option. There could be a dozen different kinds of human vermin lurking in the dark doorways on this street.

Yet if he took her inside with him and they walked into trouble...

"What are you thinking?" she asked.

"Just give me a second."

The question was, would it be trouble he couldn't handle?

Bryce and Donna. He could certainly handle them. Even if Bryce *was* a killer, he was an amateur.

Besides, if they were standing near the door, their conversation should be audible from the alley. And if they were someplace else, with any luck he and Celeste could get inside without them knowing about it.

Deciding, he said, "Want to go in? See if we can get some answers?"

She nervously licked her lips, then nodded.

"Okay, if they're right at the door we stay outside. Otherwise, the plan's to keep quiet and not let them see us."

When she nodded again, he took her hand and they headed down the dead-end alley.

As they neared the door, he put his finger to his lips and stood listening.

Not a sound.

He eased the door open an inch. There was no sign of anyone, so he drew Celeste inside with him.

The door slowly and silently swung closed behind them—but not quite all the way. He reached out to give it a shove, then stopped himself.

It was an old metal door in a frame that looked kind of warped, so it might make a huge racket if he forced it shut. And the remote possibility that some street person would wander in was the least of his concerns.

Leaving the door as it was, he turned toward Celeste. When he saw how anxious she seemed he whispered, "You okay?"

She nodded. "I just need to take a couple of deep breaths. While we were outside, I didn't realize how hard my adrenaline was pumping."

They started forward, past the battered desk that stood just inside the doorway.

An ancient phone sat on it, and absurd as it seemed considering the circumstances, the thought that she hadn't seen a rotary dial phone in years flitted through Celeste's mind. Then she focused all her attention on the moment.

If there was any heat on in the theater, the thermostat was turned down low. The air was almost as cold as the air outside, and had a musty smell. A combination of perspiration, stage makeup, stale perfume, dust and a hundred other scents.

The interior was dim; the only light in this part of the theater came from a single bulb in the hallway stretching ahead of them.

She remembered someone once telling her that a lot of old theaters were haunted by the ghosts of long-dead actors. If that was true, she'd say this one was a prime candidate.

Travis squeezed her hand as they headed quietly down the hall. Faintly, in the distance, was the sound of a radio.

As they passed a row of tiny dressing rooms, she began to hear the murmur of voices up ahead. That sent another rush of adrenaline through her.

They walked on, into the virtual darkness of the stage wing. From there, they could see Bryce and Donna standing center stage. Beyond them sat the radio, tuned to a station playing Shania Twain.

There were also a couple of props on the stage, a dining room table with a lamp sitting at one end of it—providing the only light out there.

Travis drew Celeste farther into the wing's darkness as Bryce was saying, "I don't have all night, so would you stop talking about how miserable you've been and cut to the chase?"

"Because you don't care how miserable I've been, right?"

"Donna..." he said, switching from apparent annoyance to what Celeste had always thought of as his eminently reasonable tone of voice. "I'm here, aren't I? You called me. I came. So I obviously care."

"Really. Do you think I'm an idiot?" Donna flounced across the stage, then wheeled to face him once more—looking every bit the actress.

"The only reason you came is that I threatened to kill myself if you didn't. No, let me rephrase that, because you'd probably be *happy* if I killed myself.

"The only reason you came is that I said I'd leave a letter for the managing partner of your firm. With something in it that would ruin you professionally."

"Please, Donna. Do you think I believed that? You don't *know* anything that could ruin me. There *isn't* anything."

"No? Then why *did* you come? Because you were thinking about how creative I am? Were you afraid I'd leave something for your friends? Maybe make up a juicy story about how you're the bastard of the century?"

She checked her watch, then focused on him again. "Or were you imagining an article in one of the gossip columns? About a lawyer with the staid law firm of Price, Whitechurch and Hoskins leading a perverted sex life?"

Celeste glanced at Travis. He nodded, telling her he figured that Bryce *had* come because he was afraid Donna might attack his reputation.

"Look," he said, "I'm here because I don't want us to part on bad terms. Oh, I know I said some awful things to you the other night, but if I could take them back I would."

She gave him a frigid smile. "I notice you didn't say that if you could take *me* back you would."

"Donna, I won't lie to you. We're over. There's just no way—"

"You won't lie to me? Since when? You've been lying to me all along. You're getting back together with your wife, aren't you? Just like I always knew you would."

"Don't be ridiculous."

"Ridiculous? Ha! You were in a state of shock when she left you."

"I certainly was not! I—"

"You're lying right now! You didn't even take her photograph off your desk for the first month I was living with you. Every time I went into your office, I'd see her stupid face and—"

"You had no business in my office! I told you that was the one room in the apartment I—"

"Oh, I had plenty of business in your office. You keep enough files at home that it took me weeks to go through them. But my point is you're a liar. After all the times you told me you and Celeste were finished, now you're getting back with her."

Bryce shook his head. "I don't know what gave you that idea, but—"

"Gave me that idea? How about I saw what's happening with my own eyes? How about I followed you today? Saw you go into that restaurant with a big smile plastered on your face. Saw you give her a superfriendly kiss hello."

"You followed me?" Bryce snapped. "You know, you're stark raving mad!"

"Am I," she said coldly. "Well, guess what. You're just plain stupid."

She glanced at her watch a second time,

then added, "If you'd stuck with me, you'd be getting Adele Langley's estate."

Celeste stopped breathing.

Travis's hand tightened around hers.

Bryce slowly said, "What?"

"Your 'Langley' files were the very first ones I went through," Donna told him.

"You've got a copy of Adele Langley's will. Celeste's too. And after her mother's accident, I went back and reread them carefully.

"And I started thinking that if Celeste's brother died, then Celeste died, you'd benefit a whole bunch of ways. Not only would you get the estate, you wouldn't have to go through the bother of divorcing Celeste.

"Plus, if she was dead, you'd be free to marry me right away. And we'd never have to pay her a penny in alimony."

"Are you saying *you* killed Steve Parker?" Bryce said, his voice so low that Celeste barely heard the words.

Donna shrugged. "Piece of cake."

Blinking back tears, Celeste turned toward Travis.

He was clearly as surprised as she was. But at least now they knew who'd killed her brother. And at least it hadn't been Bryce.

Why was Donna telling him she was a

murderer, though? After he'd dumped her? Was she intending to kill him, too?

When no other explanation came to mind, she looked at Travis again.

He obviously knew what was concerning her, because he touched his jacket beneath his shoulder, reminding her he was wearing his gun.

Assured that he wouldn't let things get out of hand, she turned toward the stage once more, thinking it didn't seem possible that Donna had a gun concealed anywhere. She had on spandex tights and a top that was hugging every inch it covered.

"*You* killed him," Bryce said numbly. "But how could you? You were *here* that night. In the play."

"In the *first act* of the play. I only had one scene, remember? And I didn't hang around through the second act, waiting to go out and unwind with everyone like usual.

"I took off as soon as my scene was finished. Didn't even bother getting out of makeup. Figured wearing the blond wig wouldn't be a bad idea. In case someone saw me around Steve's place."

"But...you mean..."

"Man, you can be dense, Bryce. Do I have

to spell it out word by word? I snuck into his building, arrived at his door and told him I was the woman living with you. Said I had to talk to him because Celeste had come to see us and there'd been a big scene. So he let me in to talk. And I popped him.

"I'd have done the same with Celeste, except I figured we'd both better have an alibi for when *she* got killed. So I hired a hit man."

"You what?"

"You heard me."

"Yes, but I don't believe you. Aside from anything else, you never have any money."

Donna shrugged. "I sold a few things. That diamond tennis bracelet you gave me, for one. At any rate, I was going to convince you to take me out of town for a weekend and have him kill her then.

"Of course, now that you've dumped me, there's no point in having him kill her. In fact, that's the last thing I want. It would only benefit you, and for some strange reason I've lost interest in doing that."

Bryce slowly shook his head. "Donna, why on earth have you told me all this? Do you think I'm going to keep quiet about it?"

She checked her watch yet again, then said, "I told you because you've always thought you're so much smarter than me. And I wanted you to know you're not."

"I've had it. I'm getting out of here."

"Uh-uh," she said as Bryce turned away. "Too late to escape."

He turned back. "What's that supposed to mean?"

As he spoke, Celeste felt Travis tense beside her. When she glanced at him, he pressed his fingers to her lips, then nodded, ever so slightly, in the direction of the dressing rooms.

She looked toward them and cold, raw terror seized her.

A man was there, moving silently forward—aiming an enormous gun in the direction of center stage.

She stood frozen next to Travis, certain that if they made the slightest move the man would glance over and spot them.

But he continued to stare straight ahead, his gaze not wavering while he walked closer and closer to the stage.

As he passed them, barely fifteen feet from where they were standing in the darkness, Travis slowly slid his hand under his jacket.

"What's *too late* supposed to mean?" Donna was saying. "It's supposed to mean you're a dead man. I've already paid for the contract. And since killing Celeste isn't going to do me any good, I told my man I'd changed my mind. That I wanted him to kill you, instead. He's right here, just waiting for his cue."

Within a split second, a thousand thoughts raced through Celeste's mind. The man with the gun was the Ice Man. The man who'd been paid to kill her. Who *Donna* had paid to kill her.

She sensed, rather than saw, Travis start to step forward. Then, just as he moved, Bryce dove under the table and the lamp flew off it.

The stage went black.

Travis pushed her to one side and yelled, "Police! Put down your gun or I'll—"

As the theater exploded in a roar, Travis pulled her to the floor and ordered her to stay down. Then he was gone.

TRAVIS WAS CROUCHED between the rise of the stage and the front row of seats, blanketed by the darkness and barely breathing.

He assumed Bryce and Donna were still on the stage, neither of them moving a muscle. And he knew the Ice Man had leaped off it. He'd heard the solid thud of him landing on the floor below. So he was here in the audience section somewhere. The question was, where *exactly?*

The theater was pitch-black—not even a single window to let in any moonlight. The only thing that would help him was the sound of the man moving.

But, thus far, the only sounds he'd heard were the beating of his heart and the music on the radio.

Maybe he should be glad of that, though. He could be hearing someone screaming in agony because the Ice Man's shot had hit a live target.

It could have hit Celeste.

He closed his eyes, telling himself she'd be all right. She was in the wings. The Ice Man was down here.

But he wouldn't be staying put for long. He'd want to get out of the theater.

Travis had shouted that he was police. For all their hit man knew, this place would soon be crawling with cops.

So it wasn't a matter of *if* he'd try to escape. It was which way would he head? Back to the alley or out through the main entrance?

Logic said the main entrance.

Since the alley dead-ended at the back of

the building, his only escape route was the front street. And it would be easier to head for the rear of the theater than climb back up onto the stage.

But what if the guy wasn't feeling logical?

Telling himself again that Celeste would be all right, Travis forced her image from his mind and sat listening intently.

No sound except for the radio.

So what should he do? Try to make it to the lobby before the Ice Man and intercept him there?

That struck him as the best plan. But what if he headed that way and the guy crossed him up?

If the Ice Man decided to go back out through the stage door, he'd pass right by Celeste. And if he happened to spot her…

Travis swallowed hard. Maybe he should just stay put. Then the guy couldn't get past him and up onto the stage.

Yet his gut was telling him the Ice Man would go for the easier route. And if he did that, while Travis was sitting here, he'd get away.

Praying that he was making the right decision, Travis took his phone from his pocket. He wished he could use it to call for backup, but that would be like pointing a flashlight at himself.

Besides, he had an idea. Gripping the phone like a baseball, he pitched it at the wall.

It barely hit before the theater erupted in gunfire. Shots shattered the old plaster; pieces of it noisily showered onto the floor.

In mere seconds, the excitement was over. But he knew where the shots had come from. Roughly how many rows back the Ice Man was.

As quickly and quietly as he could, he felt his way along the front row and began crab-scuttling up the far aisle, keeping his head down and praying the sound of the radio would cover his movement.

The Ice Man would probably sit tight for a minute, peering through the darkness and hoping to hear something else.

In that event, if Travis was quiet enough, he'd make it safely to the front lobby. Then it would only be a matter of waiting.

CHAPTER SEVENTEEN

Sunday, October 10, 10:03 p.m.

CELESTE EDGED CLOSER to the stage, even though trying to see was pointless. The theater was just as dark as it had been before that blast of gunshots.

Their echoes had faded now, and except for the radio all was silent again. Yet there was nothing peaceful about the silence.

In fact, she couldn't stop thinking it might mean that Travis was lying dead. That she'd lost the man she loved.

If he'd been shooting at the Ice Man, if he'd killed him, surely he'd have come to tell her. And since he hadn't…

Shaking her head, she tried to clear the fog of fear from her mind.

She really had no idea *what* had happened. Didn't know which of them had been firing. Maybe both had. And maybe…

Telling herself this was no time to play

guessing games, she tried to think. She had to do something. But what?

For a moment, she couldn't come up with a single idea. Then she remembered the phone. Sitting on that battered desk just inside the stage door.

She looked toward the dusty light drifting from the hallway. All she had to do was walk down it and call 911. And pray that the Ice Man didn't come walking down it after her.

If he did, he'd kill her. But if he did, it would mean he'd already killed Travis.

Tears stung her eyes. If he had, she didn't care whether she ended up dead or not.

She pushed herself from the floor and quietly headed toward the hall—stopping in terror as a board squeaked beneath her feet.

Not breathing, she stood listening, terrified she'd hear footsteps behind her. When she didn't, she started forward again.

As she reached the hall, she couldn't help imagining herself silhouetted in the light, a perfect target. Couldn't keep from thinking that hit men were undoubtedly excellent shots.

Aware each step she took might be her last, she reached the phone, picked it up with trembling hands and continued on to the door.

The cord was more than long enough to let her step outside.

In the alley, she dialed emergency and told the operator that a police detective and an armed killer were in the Winslow Lane Theater. That shots had been fired. That no, she didn't know the address. But it was on the street north of Bleeker, a block from Broadway.

Hanging up, she took a deep breath of cold night air, unable to keep her mind from returning to the fact that Donna had killed Steve.

She'd told him she had to talk to him; he'd let her in thinking she needed help. And he was dead because of it.

Now Travis might be dead, as well.

She set the phone down on the crumbling pavement and started toward the dark street, telling herself she wasn't going to cry. Not unless her worst fears were confirmed.

TRAVIS STOOD WITH his back pressed against one wall of the lobby. Waiting. And sweating, despite the lack of heat in the theater.

The mesh-covered glass panel in the door was almost completely covered by the *Talking Too Loud* poster, and the lobby was practically as dark as the audience section had been. Practically, but not quite.

A few faint moon shadows were making their way inside, and his eyes had adjusted well enough that he'd easily be able to see the Ice Man.

If he came this way. If he didn't decide to leave by the stage door—the route that would take him directly past Celeste.

Come on, Travis silently urged him. *Make your move. This is the exit you want.*

He was barely breathing, was totally focused on watching and listening. Then, from the distance, he heard the sound of sirens.

His pulse leaped. Had someone outside heard the shooting? Called the cops?

In this neighborhood, that wasn't likely. And the whine of sirens was common in New York City. Those cars could be on their way anywhere.

But the louder the noise got, the more likely it seemed that this was their destination.

Travis held his breath as a few more seconds passed.

The Ice Man had to be hearing the sound by now, and it would force him to act.

It did.

Suddenly, Travis heard the thudding footsteps of someone running down an aisle. But not toward the lobby!

Crap! The sirens had made the Ice Man decide the main entrance would be a mistake. That was where the squad cars would converge, so he was heading for the alley.

Travis tore across the lobby and into total blackness again. He couldn't see a thing, but he could hear the Ice Man scrambling onto the stage.

"Police!" he shouted, ducking between two rows of seats. "Stop where—"

For the second time, his warning was drowned by a blast from the Ice Man's gun. Then he was on the move once more.

Travis started after him again, telling himself that at least the guy wouldn't notice Celeste. He was too intent on getting away.

But Travis wasn't going to *let* a killer get away.

Aware he had to be nearing the stage, Travis slowed his pace. He reached it, vaulted up, then raced for the hall—smashing the single light with his gun on the way past. When he went out that alley door, he didn't want to be backlit.

The door was just ahead of him now, swinging shut.

The Ice Man was outside. But was he lurking, waiting to take a shot? Or was he already running for the street, desperate to disappear into the darkness before the squad cars arrived?

Crouching tightly against the wall, Travis shoved the door halfway open.

Nothing.

He burst through as it began to swing shut, hurtled himself across to the far side of the alley, ending up behind a stack of garbage cans.

The Ice Man hadn't waited around, though. Peering out past the cans, Travis could see him charging for the street.

The sirens were close now, screaming into the night. His backup was almost at the theater. But the Ice Man was almost out of the alley.

"Police! Stop!" Travis shouted, assuming a firing stance.

The Ice Man wheeled around, his gun drawn…and Travis pulled the trigger.

The man screamed and went down, his gun clattering to the pavement.

"Stay flat on the ground," Travis yelled. "Don't move or I'll blow your brains out!"

An instant later, headlights flashed along the street and cars were screeching to a halt.

The pool of blood forming by the Ice Man's shoulder told Travis where his shot had hit.

He raised both hands above his head and waited until the first uniforms cautiously entered the alley. Two of them pointed their guns at the Ice Man. The other two aimed theirs at him.

"I'm Detective Travis Quinn, Manhattan North Homicide," he called as calmly as he could. "This is *my* crime scene.

"I want you to cuff him," he told the officers covering the Ice Man. "Then search him for other weapons and call for an ambulance."

Looking back at the two uniforms still training their guns on him, he said, "I'm going to put down my gun and take out my badge. All right?"

As desperately as he wanted to get back inside the theater, assure himself that Celeste was really okay, he couldn't go anywhere until these men were convinced of who he was.

"All right," one of them said. "Go ahead."

He slowly set his gun on the ground, then just as slowly reached for his shield. While he was holding it out, Celeste appeared around the corner of the building—and he'd never felt more relieved.

"Get back here!" a man hollered.

The next second, he followed her into view and grabbed her arm.

"Wait a minute!" Travis called. "I want to talk to that woman. Just wait right there with her.

"Okay?" he asked the officers who'd checked his badge.

As they nodded, he said, "Fine. Now, we've got a civilian and a female perp still in the theater. On the stage, last I saw. Go in through the alley door and separate the two of them.

"It's dark inside, but there've got to be light switches someplace. I'll be in to take statements shortly. And be careful. The woman may have a weapon.

"And have some of the other officers secure the scene," he added as he started toward Celeste.

She gave him a wan smile that went straight to his heart. She might not look too steady, but they'd done it. They'd both come through this intact.

"Give us a minute," he told the officer who was holding on to her.

When the man stepped away, Travis wrapped his arms around her and held her tightly.

"It's over," he whispered.

"And it wasn't Bryce."

"No. Hank and I don't often come to the wrong conclusion, but we're not perfect. You're glad it wasn't him, aren't you."

She nodded against his chest. "If it had been...I think the fact that I'd been married to a murderer would have haunted me for the rest of my life."

He kissed the top of her head, then said, "I've got to go back inside. I'm not letting anyone else take Donna's statement."

"I'll wait for you."

"Not here. If she wants a lawyer present it'll be a while. And sitting in a squad car's no fun. So why don't I have someone drive you home."

"Home," she murmured, gazing up at him. "You mean my home, or yours?"

"How about mine?"

She smiled again, and this time it looked more as if she meant it. "Because Snoops is there, right?"

He grinned. "Sure. That's as good a reason as any."

"YEAH, YEAH," Donna muttered when Travis finished reading her her rights.

"Three people heard me admit I killed Celeste's brother and hired a hit man to whack her. Four if we count him. So I've got to be really careful I don't say anything to you that might incriminate me. It doesn't strike you as a *tad* late for me to worry?"

Travis let her sarcasm pass. If she was prepared to waive her right to remain silent it was fine with him. There were a few blanks he'd like filled in.

"How did you figure on getting away with this tonight?" he said.

When she merely shrugged, he added, "Didn't you think the police would suspect you had something to do with Bryce's death? I mean, we were aware he'd thrown you out. Or didn't you know your mother had—"

"I know exactly what she did, because I asked her to do it. I was thinking that when she told the cops she figured Bryce had murdered me, they'd toss the bastard in jail. But they weren't nearly as interested as I'd hoped."

"So she was involved in all this with you."

"No," Donna said sharply. "She only agreed to help me get even with Bryce. Try to make the cops give him a hard time. She had nothing to do with anything else. Has no idea about Celeste's brother or the hit man."

"Then let's get back to how you figured on getting away with this. Here. Tonight."

"It wouldn't have been a problem. Not if *you* hadn't shown up. When the cops questioned me, I'd have admitted that I phoned Bryce and asked him to come here—because you guys would have checked his phone records, right?"

"Right."

"So, I'd have said I called and he told me he'd had a change of heart. That he wanted to make up. And I said he should come down here and we'd talk about it.

"As for his getting killed, I'd have just claimed I didn't have a clue. That one minute we were alone, talking, and the next some guy was standing there with a gun and popped him."

"And you thought we'd just buy that?"

"No, I knew you'd be suspicious. But I didn't see how you'd be able to prove anything different. And me being with him when he died, here in the theater and all…the press I'd have gotten would have been fantastic.

"A man leaves his wife to be with the

woman he loves. They fight, then make up. But suddenly—bang, bang. He's dead and I'm heartbroken. Can you imagine the headlines?

"Beautiful actress bereft. Reconciliation goes horribly wrong. Actress's true love gunned down in theater.

"That kind of publicity is priceless. Plus, I could have sold my story to one of the tabloids."

She paused to glare at Travis, then added, "You just ruined my life, you know."

He shook his head. "Uh-uh. *You* ruined your life."

As HE DROVE HOME from the Winslow Lane Theater, Travis called Hank in Chicago—asked about his father, then told him what had happened.

"So Adele Langley's death actually was an accident," Hank said when he was done.

"Uh-huh. But it was what started Donna thinking."

"And Evan Reese had nothing to do with any of it. Except to have fixated on Celeste and be a major pain."

"Yeah, well, if he doesn't lose his fixation with Celeste—fast—I'll give him a major pain."

Hank laughed, then said, "I'm just sorry I missed the excitement. And that I won't be there to see Espizito's expression when he has to congratulate you."

Travis grinned. "I'm going to really like that part. He yanks me off the case and I end up breaking it. Even if it *was* accidentally."

"Accidentally? Sure, buddy. He's not going to believe that for a second."

"Hey, all I was trying to do was prevent Celeste from getting killed. The rest just fell into my lap. At least, that's the story he gets."

"Well, regardless of what you tell him, I'm glad it's over. So…where does this leave you and Celeste?"

"I'm just on my way home to talk about that."

"Good luck, then."

"Yeah. Thanks. See you when you're back."

Travis stuck the phone into his pocket and turned down his street.

After finding a place to park, he climbed out of the Mustang and headed for his apartment. Late as it was, when he neared the building he could see Celeste standing by the window with Snoops in her arms, watching for him.

She waved, making him feel so good he

could hardly believe it. He'd never really thought about having someone waiting for him when he came home, but it would be nice. Assuming it was the *right* someone. And Celeste was.

He took the stairs two at a time, ridiculously eager to be with her again.

When he reached the upstairs hall, she was standing in the apartment doorway—minus the cat.

He drew her inside with him and gave her a major kiss.

"So," she murmured when he let her go. "The case is all wrapped up?"

"Wrapped up and tied with a bow," he said, leading her over to the couch.

"And what will happen to Donna?" she asked as they sat down. "And the Ice Man?"

"Well, she'll be charged with your brother's murder. And for hiring the Ice Man to kill you.

"He'll be looking at attempted-murder charges for tonight. And now that we've got our hands on him, we should be able to nail him for some of his past hits.

"Donna connected with him through someone named Giovanni, a guy she chatted up in a bar. And when we find him, he'll probably be willing to plea-bargain—tell us everything he knows about the Ice Man."

"So it really *is* over."

"Your part in it is. Except for testifying at the trials."

"Then I can go back to my normal life," she murmured.

Travis brushed her hair away from her face. "I was thinking we should talk about that. About where your life goes from here, I mean. And my life."

Celeste could feel her heart racing—the way it did every time she was near Travis. And all the things she'd been thinking she had to say to him didn't seem anywhere near as important as they had while she'd been waiting.

But she knew that was just a function of his effect on her. When they were together, she didn't want to even think about the possibility of not being with him.

Gathering her resolve, she quietly said, "This happened incredibly fast between us."

"I know." He took her hands in his, and when he caught her gaze she melted a little inside. "But I don't think that falling in love fast makes it any less real."

"I don't, either. It's just…it scares me, Travis. I made a mistake with Bryce, and—"

"I'm not Bryce," he whispered, leaning closer and kissing her forehead.

"No, you're nothing like Bryce. And I never felt about him the way I feel about you."

That brought a smile to his lips. And man, she loved his smile.

"How *do* you feel about me?"

"If you haven't figured that out by now," she teased, "then you're not much of a detective."

He laughed. "So, you like me."

"Maybe it's a tiny bit more than *like*."

"Good. And Snoops seems to be okay with me. And we already decided that my family is going to love you. So considering that I'm absolutely crazy about you, I really can't see any problem here."

"Oh, Travis, maybe you're right. It's just… when I'm not with you, I start thinking this can't be for real. Then I *am* with you, and I can't seem to think at all. Does that make any sense?"

"Of course. Celeste, I used to be totally convinced that I'd never fall in love. That I'd never *let* myself. Then I met you and discovered I didn't have the slightest control over it.

"Yet that doesn't mean I've forgotten *why* I wasn't going to let myself. It still worries me that a lot of cops don't do too well in relationships. We work shifts and have trouble keeping our cases from intruding on our personal life, so we have a high divorce rate.

"But the more time I spend with you, the less serious all that seems when it comes to *us*."

"Because I have flexible hours?" she said, doing her best not to let him see she was only teasing again. "Because it would be easier for me to adjust to your schedule than for most women?"

"Very funny," he told her. Then he pulled her close and gave her a kiss.

When he finally ended it, though, he looked so serious she felt uneasy.

"There's one more thing I want to talk about," he said.

Her heart stopped. Surely there couldn't be another potential problem. One she hadn't managed to think of on her own.

"What is it?" she made herself ask.

"Well...the theory that Bryce wanted to get his hands on your mother's estate. I mean, I know we were wrong about that, but I keep wondering if you're worried that *I*... Because

I don't want any part of it. In fact, I think you should put it in some kind of trust or something and—"

She draped her arms around his neck and went back to kissing him. That *was* something she hadn't thought of on her own. But it was the last thing that would worry her.

In some respects, she felt as if she'd known Travis forever. And she just knew he wasn't a man who'd marry for money.

When she'd kissed him thoroughly enough that she was sure he had the message, she eased back and smiled.

"It's not really *that* much money, you know. I mean, it's more than I'd have thought, but when you consider I'm a freelancer, with no company pension... Let's just say it'll keep me in my old age."

He gently traced her jaw with his fingertips. "I was kind of thinking *I'd* keep you in your old age. That I'd marry you and keep you forever.

"I mean, if you think we should hold off on formalizing things for a while, we can. But I don't want to spend even one more day of my life without you."

"Oh, Travis," she whispered. She didn't want to spend even one more day of her life without him, either. And wasn't that more important than anything else could possibly be?

"Is that a yes?" he said.

She smiled again, suddenly happier than she'd ever dreamed of being.

"If you haven't figured that out by now..."

She didn't get to add the *then you're not much of a detective* bit. She couldn't speak with Travis kissing her.

* * * * *

REQUEST YOUR FREE BOOKS!
2 FREE WHOLESOME ROMANCE NOVELS IN LARGER PRINT
PLUS 2
FREE
MYSTERY GIFTS

⁂⁂⁂⁂⁂⁂⁂⁂⁂⁂⁂⁂⁂⁂⁂⁂⁂⁂

HEARTWARMING™

⁂⁂⁂⁂⁂⁂⁂⁂⁂⁂⁂⁂⁂⁂⁂⁂⁂⁂⁂⁂⁂

Wholesome, tender romances

LARGER-PRINT BOOKS!

GET 2 FREE LARGER-PRINT NOVELS PLUS 2 FREE MYSTERY GIFTS

Love Inspired®

Larger-print novels are now available...

	DATE DUE	